Television

Other books in the Careers for the Twenty-First Century series:

Aeronautics
Art
Biotechnology
Computer Technology
Education
Emergency Response
Engineering
Film
Finance
Law
Law Enforcement
Medicine
Military
Music
The News Media
Publishing

Careers
for the
Twenty-First
Century

Television

by R.T. Byrum

LUCENT BOOKS

An imprint of Thomson Gale, a part of The Thomson Corporation

Detroit • New York • San Francisco • San Diego • New Haven, Conn.
Waterville, Maine • London • Munich

For more information, contact
Lucent Books
27500 Drake Rd.
Farmington Hills, MI 48331-3535
Or you can visit our Internet site at http://www.gale.com

LIBRARY OF CONGRESS CATALOGING-IN-PUBLICATION DATA

Byrum, R.T., 1938–
   Television / by R.T. Byrum.
     p. cm. — (Careers for the twenty-first century)
Includes bibliographical references and index.
ISBN 1-59018-400-9 (alk. paper)
1. Television—Vocational guidance—Juvenile literature. I. Title. II. Series.
PN1992.55.B96 2005
791.4502'93—dc22

                                                      2004020961

Printed in the United States of America

Contents

Foreword

Young people in the twenty-first century are faced with a dizzying array of possibilities for careers as they become adults. However, the advances in technology and a world economy in which events in one nation increasingly affect events in other nations have made the job market extremely competitive. Young people entering the job market today must possess a combination of technological knowledge and an understanding of the cultural and socioeconomic factors that affect the working world. Don Tapscott, internationally known author and consultant on the effects of technology in business, government, and society, supports this idea, saying, "Yes, this country needs more technology graduates, as they fuel the digital economy. But . . . we have an equally strong need for those with a broader [humanities] background who can work in tandem with technical specialists, helping create and manage the [workplace] environment." To succeed in this job market young people today must enter it with a certain amount of specialized knowledge, preparation, and practical experience. In addition, they must possess the drive to update their job skills continually to match rapidly occurring technological, economic, and social changes.

   Young people entering the twenty-first-century job market must carefully research and plan the education and training they will need to work in their chosen careers. High school graduates can no longer go straight into a job where they can hope to advance to positions of higher pay, better working conditions, and increased responsibility without first entering a training program, trade school, or college. For example, aircraft mechanics must attend schools that offer Federal Aviation Administration–accredited programs. These programs offer a broad-based curriculum that requires students to demonstrate an understanding of the basic principles of flight, aircraft function, and electronics. Students must also master computer technology used for diagnosing problems and show that they can apply what they learn toward routine maintenance and any number of needed repairs. With further education, an aircraft mechanic can gain increasingly specialized licenses that place him or her in the job market for positions of higher pay and greater responsibility.

In addition to technology skills, young people must understand how to communicate and work effectively with colleagues or clients from diverse backgrounds. James Billington, librarian of Congress, asserts that "we do not have a global village, but rather a globe on which there are a whole lot of new villages . . . each trying to get its own place in the world, and anybody who's going to deal with this world is going to have to relate better to more of it." For example, flight attendants are increasingly being expected to know one or more foreign languages in order for them to better serve the needs of international passengers. Electrical engineers collaborating with a sister company in Russia on a project must be aware of cultural differences that could affect communication between the project members and, ultimately, the success of the project.

The Lucent Books Careers for the Twenty-First Century series discusses how these ideas come into play in such competitive career fields as aeronautics, biotechnology, computer technology, engineering, education, law enforcement, and medicine. Each title in the series discusses from five to seven different careers available in the respective field. The series provides a comprehensive view of what it is like to work in a particular job and what it takes to succeed in it. Each chapter encompasses a career's most recent trends in education and training, job responsibilities, the work environment and conditions, special challenges, earnings, and opportunities for advancement. Primary and secondary source quotes enliven the text. Sidebars expand on issues related to each career, including topics such as gender issues in the workplace, personal stories that demonstrate exceptional on-the-job experiences, and the latest technology and its potential for use in a particular career. Every volume includes an "Organizations to Contact" list as well as annotated bibliographies. Books in this series provide readers with pertinent information for deciding on a career and as a launching point for further research.

Careers in Television: Artistic, Creative, and Technical

Few industries offer a product so in demand as does television. In the United States more than 98 percent of households own at least one television set. More often than not, the television is turned on for an average of eight hours daily. Viewing habits vary from household to household, but studies show that individuals actively watch the screen at least four hours per day, or twenty-eight hours per week—more than a full day glued to the tube.

To help fulfill this demand, the television industry has an ongoing and ever increasing need for the many types of professionals it takes to produce the programming and to operate the increasingly sophisticated broadcasting equipment. There are many opportunities for a person who desires a career as a creator of program content (producing, directing, or writing) or as a member of the technical operations staff (audio or video engineer or camera operator) or as talent (actor, host, or newscaster) performing before the camera.

Added to the potential for growth in the industry is the

demand for all broadcast facilities to be upgraded to handle high-definition television and to make the switch from analog to digital technology. This opens brand new doors to persons trained to handle these newer technologies, which are rooted in the same types of knowledge and skills found in the computer industry.

A career in television is not limited to working in a commercial broadcast station. Many companies have internal communications departments complete with fully equipped television studios. Delta Airlines, for example, produces training videos and internal communications as well as the safety videos shown before takeoff on many of its aircraft.

Independent production studios produce commercials, features, documentaries, and many of the serial programs aired at local or network television stations. These companies employ persons with the same technical and creative background found in commercial broadcast facilities.

These video engineers oversee all of the video equipment on the set of the popular television series Law & Order.

A television news crew in Florida broadcasts during a hurricane. Television work can sometimes be dangerous.

Colleges and universities often use closed-circuit television to communicate with students and faculty, and they may televise certain classes to be distributed to remote classrooms or to other educational institutions. Professional staff members are needed to operate and maintain the equipment. Similar facilities are found in hospitals, military bases, large retirement communities, and even some large hotels.

Since the equipment, the operation, the talent, and the experience needed is similar, it is possible for a person to move comfortably from one segment of the television industry to another. Regardless of where a person finds a job in the industry, the reality of television is that it is mostly hard work with occasional bursts of glamour. Often an employee is called on to spend long and irregular hours to complete a production. Exposure to bad weather and unpleasant or hazardous conditions is not unusual. Pay in markets other than the major ones in Los Angeles and New York may seem low compared to the workload, but an enterprising person can climb the promotion ladder locally or improve income potential by moving from smaller to larger markets.

It is important that someone aspiring to a career in television make an initial decision regarding the field in which he or she would like to work. This is helpful in continuing education, obtaining an internship, or finding on-the-job training opportunities. High school and college counselors, books, and Internet career sites are helpful sources of information. Additionally, taking any occasion to have a written or in-person discussion with professionals in a chosen field can assist in determining a correct choice and can open doors to possible future employment.

Even with the growing prospects for working at a television station or a video production house, there will always be competition as employers seek out the best and most dedicated applicants. The earlier a person begins planning and preparing for a career, the better the chance for success.

Chapter 1

Camera Operator

One of the key positions in any television station is that of camera operator, also known as a videographer or a cameraman, a term still widely used regardless of a person's gender. That person is responsible for shooting the video or picture portion of a television broadcast. Operators of cameras with built-in or remote recorders also have the ability to add audio to the video. For news and short features, the automatic volume control of the camera or recorder makes a separate audio operator unnecessary.

The decision to become a videographer frequently begins with a person's attraction to photography as a youth. A photographer's attention to detail, including lens characteristics, lighting, framing, and the instinct for capturing emotion and action, is a skill needed by both still and motion camera operators. Added to those basics, the videographer captures the motion and sound expected by the television viewing audience.

In addition to a love of photography, the person actively seeking a career as a camera operator may be attracted by the excitement of working with on-camera talent or by the adventure of on-location assignments covering sports, news, or special events. Thanks to satellite relays, the camera operator has the opportunity to share live events on the other side of the city or of the world with viewers at home.

David Hand, a professional with a long and distinguished career, has experienced both the glamour and the hard work of being a videographer. He believes that the desire and dedication required for the position make it more than just a job:

You know that this is what you are meant to do in life. Being a cameraman is not a job but it is a lifestyle. The life must suit you; the work must not be work for you. You must have a love-hate relationship with it. There must be days that you think of nothing else that you should be doing in life and there must be days that you wish you worked in a bank.

At an Olympic basketball game in 1996, a camera operator sits on a dolly to film players sitting on the bench at eye level.

I always thought that if someone asks, "How do I become a cameraman?" then they have failed already. It is not a job and it is more than a passion. How does someone become a painter, a sculptor, or an artist?[1]

Station managers look for people with Hand's drive, skills, knowledge, and the ability to do the work with minimum supervision. They want applicants with an eye for a good picture, imagination, and creativity as well as a good technical understanding of how the camera operates. Competition is high for the limited number of positions. Stations can afford to pick the best, and they usually are not willing to do formal on-the-job training. Fortunately for the aspiring videographer, there are proven steps that can help open the door to a career in this rewarding field.

Preparing Through Formal Education

The most promising applicant for the camera operator's position likely has a background that includes a degree in broadcast com-

Cameraman or Director of Photography

In television, there are two distinct types of camera operators, usually designated as either a cameraman or a director of photography (DP). The cameraman generally works on a multi-camera show, such as in-studio programming, sports coverage, or special events (parades, convention coverage, etc.), or covers news events with a portable camcorder. The scenes are shot using either natural lighting or light from a single lamp. The skill and experience level determines the pay rate, but cameramen earn around thirty-two thousand dollars on average. In contrast, a director of photography is highly skilled in multiple cameras and lights to achieve dramatic and special effects. DPs command a higher pay rate of fifty thousand dollars and up for their technical and artistic expertise, and they usually work freelance, moving from project to project. Although a cameraman may acquire the training to become a director of photography, most DPs set their goals and base their training on that advanced career path from the beginning.

These aspiring camera operators are studying video production. Camera operators typically have a degree in broadcast communication.

munication. Classroom instruction at accredited colleges, universities, and broadcast schools covers technical instruction on operating television cameras and the associated equipment needed to originate programming. Additional courses deal with the creative end of the industry: producing, directing, script writing, set design, lighting and sound effects, acting, and voice-over announcing.

The preferred curriculum will also include hands-on experience in the institution's fully equipped television studio and on outside assignments using portable recorder/camera systems. Students learn how to effectively cover live action and how to work with talent. They are taught what they are expected to do when the director calls for close-ups, or head shots; medium, or two, shots; or crowd, or wide, shots. They practice moving the camera forward and backward (called dollying), side to side (trucking), panning (swinging the camera left and right), tilting the camera up or down, and smoothly zooming the lens in and out. With repetition, the student learns to respond automatically to a director's call for any of these actions.

Accredited schools and colleges not only prepare students for work in television, but many also offer help in finding permanent jobs. Even before promising students graduate, the school may arrange for internships at local television stations.

An Internship in Camera Work

An internship at a television station provides training under actual work conditions. The duties can involve working in the prop and set department, assisting the lighting director, operating the teleprompter, or functioning as the floor manager, the person who receives the program director's commands over a headset and relays them by cue cards or hand signals to the on-camera talent to indicate timing and pace. The floor manager's position is especially useful in understanding how a camera operator and the rest of the production team work together.

Since the floor manager works closely with the camera operators, the job is sometimes considered a stepping-stone to the operator's position. By listening to the commands that the program director gives to the camera operators and by observing their responses, the floor manager gains the knowledge that will help in landing a camera operator's position. The experience obtained through an internship, the coaching offered by professionals in the field, and the opportunity to establish contacts can result in full-time employment after graduation.

Breaking into the television industry is rarely easy, but following a course of study that includes practical training is a proven means of becoming a television camera operator. A well-written résumé and letters of reference from clients, teachers, and employers are usually needed for any job-hunting venture, but the serious aspiring videographer should also compile a show reel. A show reel is a videotape containing samples of work in which the prospective employee has taken an active part in shooting. In a competitive field like videography, a well-done show reel can make the difference in finding that first job.

Serving as an intern can be more than just an important step in landing a job, though. Not only does the internship place a person in contact with influential people in the business, but it also offers the opportunity to experience a typical workday within the television environment.

A Day in the Life of a
Television Camera Operator

Working conditions for camera operators vary considerably, but those employed in studios operated by government agencies, corporations, advertising agencies, or television and cable networks usually work a five-day, forty-hour week. By contrast, field camera operators, frequently referred to as videographers, may work long, irregular hours and must be available for duty on short notice. Those who cover major events, such as conventions, parades, or sporting events, often travel. They may stay overnight on short assignments or be away for longer periods if assigned to cover events in more distant locales.

Outdoor productions can present challenging working conditions. Both operator and camera might need protection against the weather. Depending on the time of day, conditions may call for using a multitude of portable lights, lens filters, reflectors, or shades. In addition, noisy surroundings can make it difficult to hear the director's commands.

A field camera operator gets ready to shoot the start of a baseball game. Outdoor productions are often very challenging for videographers.

Television

Many types of video cameras are needed to meet the different requirements of live or recorded programming, but all camera operators share common backgrounds and duties. The typical day begins with checking out equipment that may have been used by other operators. Batteries must be charged, lenses and cables examined, and, since electronic components deteriorate with age or behave differently depending on temperature conditions, the camera must be adjusted before each use. This routine includes resetting the white, black, and color levels to match broadcast standards.

Shooting assignments are posted, and the day's schedule may include briefings, rehearsals, and on-air programming. Each operator is responsible for assembling and checking the equipment and for arriving on time at the shooting location.

Before an actual shoot, especially with a scripted program, there is often a run-through, or rehearsal. Even so, the best-rehearsed show may have unexpected deviations that require the operator to make split-second decisions to work around the problem. For example, in a multicamera sequence, if one camera malfunctions, the remaining camera operators will then be

Although The Young and the Restless *is a rehearsed program, this camera operator is ready for any deviations from the script.*

asked to fill in for the missing camera. The director must then depend heavily on the camera operators to move quickly, compose unscheduled shots, and follow action not covered in their rehearsal.

The Duties of the Studio Camera Operator

Although many tasks and experiences are common to both studio and field camera operators, the studio camera operator's day differs significantly from that of the field videographer. Still, the studio operator's work varies from day to day.

Art Kibby, co-owner of Kibby Raynor Productions and its primary camera operator, describes the different types of shoots in his studio:

> Our productions range from product demonstrations, to training videos, talk shows, travel features, and, occasionally, commercials. The variety of programs demands a high degree of skill and experience to cope with the changing conditions. We also shoot videos for focus groups. That's where we videotape a cross-section of consumers who rate products according to effectiveness and appeal. We also do blue screen videos where the actor stands in front of a blue background and we insert a virtual set behind him, similar to the way weather forecasters are shown in front of a changing weather map. Saves a lot of travel time and expense when you can put a person in a beach chair and have them appear in Florida without leaving the studio.[2]

Prior to the broadcast or taping, the operator will receive a script briefing to establish which camera will be responsible for certain angles and scenes. Movements and actions like panning, tilting, dollying, and zooming are rehearsed in a prebroadcast run-through. A shot-sheet with those actions specified is usually taped to the camera or tripod so the operator can prepare for the next scene in advance.

The studio camera is a large piece of equipment, and maneuvering it smoothly is a major requirement of any operator. The typical studio equipment consists of the camera body, a zoom lens, and a small video monitor on a swivel mounted above the camera. The unit sits on a pan head fitted with two handles like a bicycle, allowing the camera to swing left and right. The pan head in turn attaches to the top of either a tripod or an adjustable pedestal. All of this rests on a dolly with casters or wheels. Electrical and mechanical controls to zoom and focus the lens are located on the handles. In addition, a boom microphone mounted on a movable dolly may be used in the production, presenting yet another obstacle to work around. The ability to maintain good picture composition while maneuvering a camera around obstructions is the mark of the professional studio camera operator.

During a taping or a live broadcast, the operator is under the command of the program director by means of a two-way headset. This allows the director to ask for minor adjustments in the picture: tilt up, zoom out, or pan left, for example. Still, the camera operator is expected to anticipate what the director wants and to deliver it when it is needed. The opportunity to ask for instructions is limited. Once the on-air light is illuminated, the conversation between camera operator and director is mostly one way since studio microphones could pick up the operator's voice. Moreover, not every shot or movement is at the director's command. During loosely scripted programming, the camera operators may be given license to compose their own pictures. The director will ask them to provide interesting situations and angles. An experienced operator can do much to improve a show and to help the director by providing such candid shots.

On rare occasions the studio camera operator may be assigned to do a location production. Examples include shooting a commercial at a car dealership or covering special events like parades or election-night celebrations. For this reason, even studio camera operators must be prepared to cope with conditions such as rain, snow, or bright sun. Controlling the lighting on a subject, coping with unwanted background noise, being able to solve technical and production problems in the field, and having the ability to work with a wide range of talent and directors are part of the job.

In most instances, however, outdoor and location work is assigned to a field camera operator, for whom challenging conditions are something to face every day.

Specialized Camera Mounts

Camera operators who shoot made-for-television movies, dramatic series, and commercials often use sophisticated equipment not found in a typical television station. Although the video cameras may be similar, the mounting systems and shooting techniques resemble those used in movie studios. For example, the camera operator's seat and the camera are mounted on a dolly, or a wheeled cart set on rails. The operator shoots the scene as assistants roll the cart along the track. The camera and operator are sometimes located on a long, counterbalanced arm called a boom crane, which helpers tilt up or down and pan left or right to follow the action. The Steadicam is a camera-mount harness equipped with springs and counterbalances worn by an operator to provide a steady picture even as the operator moves through the scene with the actors. A more complex version of the Steadicam may be mounted in a helicopter, boat, or wheeled vehicle when the script calls for that type of coverage. The special skills needed to effectively use such equipment command higher pay than those of operators of simple tripods and pedestal-mounted cameras in television studios.

A camera operator uses a Steadicam to film Maurice Green's victory salute at a 2004 Olympic track event.

The Duties of a Field Camera Operator

Unlike the studio operator, the electronic news gathering camera operator or production videographer can virtually have the world as his or her stage. Most of the work is done away from the

President Bush speaks with reporters at an outdoor news conference. Assignments for news camera operators are often exciting.

television station. Assignments are rarely routine, often exciting, sometimes filled with danger, but are usually rewarding. Yura Monestime, a camera operator in Ontario, Canada, who refers to his work as visual art, illustrates this point in writing about the highlights of his wide-ranging career as a videographer:

> I traveled extensively covering elections, international stories, and papal, presidential, and monarchal visits. I was in Florida to film the launch of the first Canadian in space, Marc Garneau. I was in Washington when [then–Soviet leader Mikhail] Gorbachev came to visit the United States for the first time. I spent time in Buckingham Palace while filming a Commonwealth Conference. I met [South African leader Nelson] Mandela when he visited Ottawa. I witnessed [Canadian prime minister Pierre] Trudeau's resignation and filmed his goodbye party. Since I have covered

four elections, I have been in nearly every small town in Canada. Life as a cameraman has taken me 3,000 feet in the air shooting aerobatics for the Snowbirds, and 6,000 feet underground filming mining practices. I embrace the challenge.[3]

A videographer works with a camcorder, which combines a video camera and an audio/video recorder in one unit. Depending on the action to be taped, the camcorder can be handheld, placed on a tripod, or shoulder mounted. The camcorder has both a directional microphone, which is mounted next to the lens for recording background audio, and an auxiliary input for a wired or wireless microphone if a person is being videotaped.

Camera operators, especially those covering accidents, natural disasters, civil unrest, or military conflicts, may be forced to work in uncomfortable or even dangerous surroundings. More often, however, there may be long periods of waiting for a newsworthy event to occur. Independent producer and cameraman Paul Thorman notes the less glamorous aspects of the working conditions as well as a few of the rewards:

> Patience is an important trait for the profession. Electronic field production operators, we go by EFP to simplify things, often work under strict deadlines, yet, many camera operators must wait long hours for an event to take place and must stand or walk for long periods while carrying multiple pieces of equipment. That being said, the satisfaction of doing your best under difficult conditions, and then hearing your work being praised by clients and viewers makes it all worthwhile.[4]

The operator must be able to do the job in spite of conditions and surroundings. A shoot may occur when excited or unruly crowds can be a threat to the operator and the equipment. While covering such an event, the videographer must remain focused but must also be prepared to flee to safety.

Videographers sometimes witness tragedies during assignments. Keeping personal feelings in check while recording events is difficult, but it is part of the job. Forty-one-year-old Joseph

McCarthy, a New York–based freelance videographer, describes his own arrival at the World Trade Center following the terrorist attack on September 11, 2001:

> After hearing of the attack, I diverted from my assignment and headed downtown. The sight that greeted me on the way down was incomprehensible. Police officers watched the World Trade Center burn as people jump to their deaths. I moved closer as the towers burned furiously. The heat was so intense that I could actually hear the building melting. I moved right across the street and shot this shot, then stopped rolling. Seconds later, the building collapsed and I was running for my life. Immediately after the first collapse, I had run back when the building started falling and was trapped against One World Financial Center with a bunch of police and fire personnel. As the debris cloud hit like a freight train and the building came crashing down around us, we cowered there helpless and unable to move. I thought that was it, as I could no longer breathe, everything went black, and I just prayed that it wouldn't hurt too much. Then one of the NYPD officers shot the window out and we all spilled in panic into that lobby, then frantically tried to escape from it as there was no air at all. I dropped my camera, but when we were able to smash our way out the other side, I went back in and retrieved it, and just started rolling in a daze, choking and gagging on the ash and smoke.[5]

Some assignments call for specialized skills and cameras. Production and news helicopters, for example, have a camera in a movable turret mounted beneath the aircraft. The camera operator sits in the cabin and remotely controls the turret and camera with a joystick. In other instances, the operator may even be called on to use special cameras designed for underwater shoots or hidden cameras for covering investigative stories.

Videographers are people who not only love making pictures but also thrive on the adventure, excitement, and glamour of their career. Even the downside of occasional danger, uncomfortable working conditions, and limited pay will not discourage those who dedicate their lives to the job.

Camera Operators in Danger

Camera operators work in a world filled with pockets of danger. Some assignments, such as covering events in the Middle East, can put operators in harm's way. This excerpt, taken from an article entitled "How Cameramen Protect Themselves While Covering Riots," is from the TV Cameramen Web site:

While in the field we use two types of armour, light and heavy. Light armour is a light stab-proof jacket that weighs almost nothing and a plastic helmet. That armour is used when we are behind the Israeli forces and the only threat is stones and Molotov bombs. With light armour you are a lot more flexible and can move faster. Heavy armour is a bullet-shrapnel proof jacket (that weighs a few kilos) and a Kevlar helmet that should, in theory, stop a bullet. The heavy armour is used when we judge that there is shooting with live or rubber bullets. The helmets are also heavier than the plastic ones, so you may end up with a nasty headache after wearing one for a while but not as big a headache as you would get if you got hit by a bullet without the helmet.

The camera is protected by the Portabrace and the lens is fitted with a UV filter. There is nothing more you can do for that.

We never go alone somewhere and the people we are with are people that we know and trust. But most important is that we evaluate every situation when we are there and we never take any unnecessary risks.

Covering skirmishes between Israelis and Palestinians, these camera operators are wearing heavy helmets and jackets as protection.

The Future and Earnings

The positive side of the income issue is that there are good prospects for higher pay either by moving to larger markets or by being promoted due to improved skills and experience. In addition, more openings are being created as television communication expands. Recent statistics show that American television stations currently employ approximately ten thousand video camera operators. As new stations are established, it is predicted that another fifteen hundred operators will be needed by 2010.

Careers in broadcasting are sought more for the glamour and excitement than for the income. The median annual wage for television studio and field camera operators was $32,720 in 2002. Incomes vary according to the sales potential of the broadcast coverage area, the size and earnings of the production house or television station, and the skills and qualifications of the operator.

Moving Up

Advancement may involve a camera operator transferring to a bigger station. Such a change may mean relocating to an entirely different part of the state or nation. In order to gain a pay increase without moving, a camera operator may elect to accept a management position. Some camera operators become directors of photography, for example. Others supplement their income by teaching full or part time at technical schools, film schools, or universities.

A person entering and remaining in this specialized field, whether identified as a camera operator, cameraman, or videographer, is an artist. The career requires a dedication that looks beyond sometimes difficult assignments and an income that may not match the workload. Even so, those who make the job their life's work agree that the satisfaction of a job well done and the fascination with the work make it all worthwhile.

Chapter 2

Director

The television director, whether assigned to entertainment or news programs, is responsible for making creative decisions regarding a production, expressing ideas, and creating images from the writer's script to entertain, inform, or instruct an audience. Directors not only interpret and approve the scripts, but they also have a say in the choreography and the music when applicable.

To be successful, the director needs flexibility and organizational skills as well as a great amount of patience. That involves working with actors of all types and ages and striving to help them deliver flawless performances while occasionally working under undesirable and unpleasant conditions. The director organizes rehearsals and meets with writers, designers, financial backers, and production technicians. Additional pressure comes from the need to adhere to budget constraints, union work rules, and production schedules.

Directors must be tough and decisive. They are accountable for virtually every phase of a program, from the initial planning to preproduction meetings overseeing technical details, conducting rehearsals, directing the program, and supervising the postproduction editing. They are heavily involved in arranging the shooting schedules and are under strict deadlines. They are also in charge of the on-screen talent, the writers, the camera operators, the broadcast engineers, and all of the lighting and staging technicians needed to produce a program.

Laurent Minassian, a director at News Channel 8 and ABC affiliate WJLA 7 in the Washington, D.C., area, understands the importance of having regard for the people who take direction from him. Each person is an artist and deserves to be treated with respect. He explains his attitude toward them:

A director and his crew ensure that everything is ready as television news anchors prepare to go on the air.

As a director I feel it is my responsibility to motivate the crew and to get them excited about the show. When it comes to directing, I want the show to be perfect. I call my cues fast, but at the same time I am very clear on what I need. It may seem standard to give the ready cues, but I have seen directors just give the commands, without a ready or a stand by, and this makes it stressful on the crew especially when working with a new crew, so I strive to be as clear as possible. I have directed all kinds of events: interviews, talk shows, sports, dancers, singers, special events, etc. Because I can run a camera I understand what a camera operator goes through to move a camera. I always give the operator enough time to get the shot ready. Because I know the camera, the operator also respects what I go through when I direct. Since we both understand each other's positions, there is a certain respect between the camera operator and me. This is the same for the other production positions.[6]

A sense of timing is another vital quality, especially for a director of live broadcasting. These individuals work under constant pressure from the need to operate with strict adherence to schedules—right down to the second for commercial programming. A master log is kept to show when each commercial is inserted and when each station break is executed. In order to keep every element on schedule, the director knows, to the second, how much time there is between breaks to make sure the people appearing on-air deliver their content.

During the taping—or in the case of live programming, the actual broadcast—the director cues the performers as to when to make entrances and informs the technicians on light, sound, or set changes. When a taped program is completed, the director will be involved in the editing process. During live broadcast, when an unexpected event occurs, such as the failure of a camera or a missed cue, the director must be able to make quick decisions to keep the program on track. There is no such word as *cut* when a live show is on the air.

Marita Grabiak has been directing episodes of prime-time television dramas such as *Wonderfalls* since February 2000. During an interview, she explained how a director's stress level can be raised by having to keep track of the many details of a production: "The director can be overwhelmed by a lot of things in the scene: the lighting, the acting, the words, the camera moves. The more detail-oriented you are as a person, the better a director you're going to be."[7] Grabiak notes that challenges multiply as the director moves from show to show. Grabiak's ability to adjust to the demands of the different types of programming has resulted in a rewarding career. The proof lies in her list of credits, which includes a number of high-rated programs: *ER, Angel, Buffy the Vampire Slayer, Smallville*, and many others.

Such flexibility allows a director to maximize his or her learning. One of the greatest directors of all time was Elia Kazan, whose classic screen works included *A Streetcar Named Desire* and *On the Waterfront*. Addressing students at Wesleyan University in Connecticut, he spoke about the qualities and life experiences that make a good director. He described the common dedication to learning involved in any directing career, whether in film or television:

Do not think, as you were brought up to think, that education starts at six and stops at twenty-one, that we learn only from teachers, books and classes. For (directors) that is the least of it. The life of a director is a totality and he learns as he lives. Everything is pertinent; there is nothing irrelevant or trivial. Lucky Man, to have such a profession! Every experience leaves its residue of knowledge behind. Every book we read applies to us. Everything we see and hear; if we like it, we steal it. Nothing is irrelevant. It all belongs to us.[8]

Although the most successful directors are always learning, some of the traits such as creativity, a sense of timing, patience, decisiveness, and people skills, are not so much learned as they are inborn. Technical skills can be taught, but these have little value if the person in the director's chair lacks the instincts for the job. As evidence that innate talent, rather than learned skills, is the key to success, an increasing number of directors are coming from the ranks of writers, actors, and actresses who possess similar traits and want to use their writing and acting experience to direct others.

Education

A formal education, then, may not be a prerequisite for an aspiring director. Some television stations consider previous experience in the field, show reels, and recommendations from those who know an applicant and give those factors more weight than a college degree. Given the limited number of openings in the field, however, an associate or college degree can be an asset when several talented people are competing for the same position. Larger organizations, such as television networks or production houses, are more likely to demand a degree as a qualification.

Students who choose formal training in preparing for a directing career will study the many aspects of media production, including basic video and audio technology, writing, editing, and production planning, in addition to directing techniques. Additional courses in budget management and drama are also important subjects. Usually, colleges offering courses for potential directors emphasize real-world experience over theory. Professionals who are currently working in the industry teach

Director Rodrigo Garcia (center) relaxes between scenes on the set of Six Feet Under. *Once filming begins, he monitors production with an eagle eye.*

many of the courses. For those attending colleges in Los Angeles or New York, the instructors may even be award-winning directors, and the course may well be taught on location in a network studio.

The educational institutions with the most valuable directing programs include access to a modern studio. Spending time in the director's chair prepares a person for the fast pace of commercial broadcasting. One of the requirements of most college and university telecommunications programs is the creation of a short video. Whether the assignment is to create a dramatic, a news report, a documentary, or a short entertainment feature, such projects represent an excellent opportunity for a fledgling director. Not only is the experience valuable for its own sake, but having a polished video in hand to show a potential employer could be a tiebreaker in competition for a job.

Internships in Television
Stations and Production Studios

Upon graduation, many higher education institutions offer to help in job placement through their established contacts in the industry. Even before graduation, however, the college or university can assist in another practical way by arranging an internship. Generally speaking, however, only small production houses and local broadcast or cable television stations offer internships in television direction. In fact, an internship may well involve working as a floor director—the same position that aspiring camera operators find so valuable. Just as the would-be camera operator does, the budding director learns the commands and the subsequent actions those commands elicit.

The Duties of a Floor Manager

One of the more valuable entry-level jobs that leads to becoming a program director is to serve as a floor manager (also known as a floor director). Prior to a program, the floor manager ensures that the microphones, sets, props, and technical equipment are working, are safe to use, and are in the right place. Floor managers are also responsible for audiences (if one exists) being seated and briefed on what is expected of them. The preshow briefing includes safety instructions, explains the timing of show segments, what to expect during the program, and, if recorded, when the program will be aired. In a studio setting, the floor manager is the essential link between the director in the booth and the floor below. When on the air, the director relays instructions through an earpiece to the floor manager, who then passes on timing cues to the presenters and guests and indicates to them which camera to face. Assignments can also take place at outside broadcasts, such as sporting events or parades. The floor manager may assist in the early stages of the planning and preparation of a production, act as the director's eyes and ears on the floor during the program, and be expected to handle any unforeseen problems (dead microphone, tangled cables, missing prop, etc.) in a calm and confident manner.

A fortunate intern may get a chance to call the shots and direct the control room during station breaks or during early morning shows. This involves following a script that shows what commercials and live studio shots will be displayed and the timing of each.

Aside from floor directing, there is another position that can provide a great opportunity for employment after graduation: script supervisor. This position has the advantage of giving an intern the chance to work closely with a director. Grabiak offers this advice to the graduate of a communications program who is aiming for a career in directing:

> Perhaps the best way to segue into directing is to be in close physical proximity to a director. You can't get much closer than the script supervisor, who sits next to a director on a set, watching the action in a scene on monitors that show what the camera sees. I've worked as script supervisor on many productions functioning as an additional set of eyes for the director.[9]

The Duties of a Television Director

Moving from formal education to an internship not only opens the door to a real directing position but also allows the student a preview of the duties and daily routines of a television director.

Directors fall into four general categories: staff or programming, newscast, sports, and series. All categories of directing share some common routines. For each, the day usually begins by reviewing the previous day's work. A meeting with staff and on-camera talent may also include a discussion of problems encountered in a previous show and improvements to be made. Next comes a briefing on the day's assignments and on any conditions that may affect the broadcast or taping session.

At this point the daily routines diverge. For the programming director (PD), the rest of the day will be spent in the control room calling the station breaks. Of the different types of directing, this is the most routine. Sitting in a darkened control room, the PD faces a wall of television monitors that are used to display the input from studio cameras, remote vans, video tape players, network feeds, and two large monitors for program

Sitting in the studio control room, a television director and a technician monitor the many cameras covering a news broadcast.

(what is currently on air) and for preview (what is the next bit of programming to be aired).

As with the news, sports, and series directors, the PD follows a script or the log to determine the next segment and then will either select the required source by controlling the video switcher personally or by giving the command to an engineer.

As the time to air a newscast approaches, a director with experience in working the news will usually take over for the PD. Before the broadcast the director will be given a copy of the news script to insert notes about which camera will be used in each segment and which news clips and commercial tapes are to be played and when. This type of directing is also fairly routine. The directing procedures do not vary from day to day unless there is a breaking story to be covered. Even then, certain guidelines exist that help the director maintain control over the quality of the broadcast.

Although news directors like Minassian have to employ a certain amount of artistry in their work, directing a newscast from a fixed location control room is still less demanding than directing a series or sports program. For one thing, there is no need for rehearsals—the immediacy of the news program does not allow time for them. On-air personalities usually occupy the same positions for every program, so camera shots remain much the same from day to day. The director's main concern during a newscast is not so much with the verbal content as it is with giving the proper technical cues in order to match the visuals with the news story.

Content is, for the most part, not the news director's worry. Most of the scripting and graphics decisions are made by the

Single- Versus Multicamera Directing

One basic distinction in television production exists between single-camera (film-style) and multicamera work. In single-camera production, each shot is staged individually, allowing precise camera positioning and lighting. Repeated "takes" are shot until the director is satisfied with the results. The action is often filmed or taped out of sequence based on a logical sequence of setups for the camera and lighting. For instance, there may be several scenes that take place in a particular room, but these scenes are separated by a number of minutes in the finished production. In a single-camera shoot, all action scenes taking place on that set are shot one after another. Actors must break their performance into noncontinuous bits that still appear coherent when assembled later in the editing room. In this type of production, then, performance is adjusted to fit the visual scheme.

In contrast to single-camera style, multicamera television production requires that the visual scheme be adjusted around the performance. The on-camera talent deliver their performances in real time, and the visualization is created by switching among a series of cameras trained on the unfolding event (and, in many cases, among several channels of electronically stored graphics). All "live" programs, including news and sports broadcasts, are produced this way. So, too, are talk, discussion, and game shows, which are shot "live to tape" and are then later broadcast with minimal editing. Directing in these genres offers less opportunity for creativity.

anchor, the news editor, or the reporters. The director's focus is more on timing, calling cues, and maintaining a standard look for the program. At the same time, the director must be able to handle breaking news and weather bulletins.

In contrast, the sports director must be able to call the shots from a variety of mobile vans or control rooms at dozens of sporting locations and must be able to react to the changes that take place so quickly in most sports. In addition, the director must be familiar enough with the sport being telecast to understand where the focus of action will be at any given time. Barbara S. Morris, a sportscast director at the University of Michigan, portrays the greatest challenge of directing a sportscast:

> To the television audience, watching a sportscast simply means watching an event "live" and having that event fleshed out by human, historical, and statistical information that clarifies or enlivens the contest. But for people who select and present the action—shaping it into a dramatic whole—split-second decisions are constantly made about what to include in the sports text and when to do so.[10]

During a typical live network sports production, the director has two concurrent responsibilities. First, the director must electronically guide the game coverage of a number of on-site camera operators. Second, he or she must choose the proper shot from among monitors displaying each of the on-site camera feeds, those images that are coordinated with the sportscaster's descriptions. In fulfilling these dual responsibilities, a sports director is concerned with more than game action alone. Other stories related to it must be tracked by cameras and, if selected, woven into a coherent, compelling telecast.

Ultimately, the director fashions all available live game-related stories into a sportscast. The on-site director decides instantaneously in what order and in what manner images are broadcast. Television sports directors have considerable latitude in determining what and how content is to be presented. In other words, a sports director selects and shapes available imagery into a visual interpretation of events and, in this sense, can be considered an author.

A camera operator covers the action on a football field as the director (left) coordinates the live cameras covering the event.

The series director's day is somewhat different from those of the news and sports directors. There may be a meeting with the cast to walk through the script or program lineup to map out the actors' movements while reading the lines and to organize schedules for any rehearsals. Next, the director and assistants will meet with lighting, video, and audio technicians; set designers; and camera operators on behind-the-scenes preparation. Then come the rehearsals, in which the actors and actresses and the creative and technical staff work together to bring the script to life. During a rehearsal, the director can—and does—occasionally stop the action to make adjustments or corrections in order to polish the production.

Regardless of the type of program being broadcast, the director is responsible for filing the log that verifies that all commercials were played as scheduled and for reporting any technical problems to the proper maintenance people. Before leaving for the day, the director sets up the next morning's agenda, approves or amends the cast and crew scheduling, and, in the case of a programming or newscast director, leaves messages with information that the person following on the next shift might need.

Preparing for a Shoot

A director begins working on a show well before the videotaping or live broadcast begins. A good example is the preproduction planning for a program featuring a symphony orchestra. Sitting down with a recording of the piece by the orchestra, the director listens to the piece to be performed, marking up a copy of the conductor's score with colored pens and highlighters. Segments are labeled in which solo instruments, or the brass, string, or woodwind sections are featured. Tympani, cymbals, and other percussion parts are highlighted. Wide shots of the orchestra, cutaways of the audience during applause, and shots of the conductor from the orchestra's view are all planned and noted between the featured instruments.

Then the director determines the composition of the shot (medium, close up, or wide-angle) required to show each segment as the music progresses. With a diagram of the orchestra and the stage, the director, with the help of the technical staff, determines the number and placement of cameras needed to capture the desired shots. The location of equipment must take into account cabling, platforms needed to raise the cameras above the audience, and steps to be taken in order to avoid being a distraction to the performers and the people who paid to attend the concert.

Finally, the director listens again to the music while picturing in his or her mind the different cameras and shots before being satisfied and giving the go-ahead for setting up for the real thing.

Salaries and Promotions

Despite the director's hard work, much of the credit, glamour, and rewards for a successful program go to the on-camera talent. Still, the choice of directing as a career is often based more on a passion for creativity than on pay. The average salary of a program director is thirty-five thousand dollars a year, and those starting out may earn as little as half that much.

Typically, the salary for directors who run television newsrooms in the United States is around $50,000. That is more than the average anchor, but frequently less than a station's star anchor. A lot also depends on the news director's experience, the size of the market, and the size of the production staff. In smaller markets with smaller staffs, the news director might make about $30,000, whereas the same position at one of the top network affiliates—where the staff may number close to one hundred—might command more than $100,000. By contrast, experienced directors in the entertainment field can take home $160,000 or more.

Expanding cable and satellite television operations and continued growth and development of interactive media, such as direct-for-Web movies and videos, should increase demand for directors. Employment of directors is expected to grow by 10 to 20 percent, or about as fast as average for all occupations through 2012.

Minassian sums up how he feels about having pursued directing as his life's work:

> I truly enjoy directing and I'm glad I chose it as a career. When I direct, I feel like an artist, I have a blank piece of paper (a blank tape) and I begin drawing to create a final picture (the show). Also, I enjoy the challenge of juggling multiple cameras, VTR [videotape recorder] decks, cues, talent, sets, and the other different factors. The most satisfaction comes at the end of a show when the production crew, producer, and talent are happy with the quality of the show.[11]

Chapter 3

Producer

The television producer is like an entrepreneur within the television industry, able to operate in much the same manner as the owner and president of his or her own company. Although the medium's technical complexity demands that any television program be a collective product involving many talents and decision makers, in American television the producer frequently serves as the decisive figure in shaping a program.

In every television production, the producer is the boss, according to Gary Reynolds, an award-winning senior producer at a U.S. television station. He should know, having taught television production at the college level. He points out that producers "have the power to make or break million-dollar careers, and the vision to see a project through from idea to TV broadcast."[12]

The job as a producer is to look beyond overnight ratings to long-term success and to reach beyond glitz to substance. The object is to empower citizens by informing or entertaining them. To reach audiences, the producer must first engage their attention with compelling material, presented in a form that makes sense.

The North Carolina Job Opportunities Web site explains that the producer's job is complex and multifaceted:

> (The) work requires a complete understanding of television production methods and techniques associated with the planning and execution of television programs. Even though the work does not require (the understanding of the subject of a program) in some instances, producers must be able to translate this material for use on television employing several television production concepts and theories.[13]

Producers assume direct responsibility for an individual show's overall quality and continued viability as something audiences will watch. Programs requiring a producer usually involve acting, large budgets, location shooting, or special sets and effects. Conventional wisdom in the industry consequently labels television "the producer's medium"—in contrast to film, where the director is frequently regarded as the key formative talent in the execution of a movie.

The producer's job includes managing the business and financial decisions of a made-for-television feature, sports event, newscast, or special-event programming. The responsibilities range across the boundaries of business, legal, creative, and technical issues. The work involves selecting scripts, approving the development of ideas for production, arranging financing, and determining the size and cost of the endeavor.

The U.S. Department of Labor's Bureau of Labor Statistics describes the skills and responsibilities usually expected of producers:

Producer Mark Burnett is the creator of the hit reality-television show Survivor. Producers are responsible for the quality of all programming.

Producers hire or approve the selection of directors, principal cast members, and key production staff members. They also negotiate contracts with artistic and design personnel . . . and guarantee payment of salaries, rent, and other expenses. . . . They may research material, write scripts, and oversee the production of individual pieces. Producers in any medium coordinate the activities of writers, directors, managers, and agents to ensure that each project stays on schedule and within budget.[14]

The Cable News Network (CNN), in advertising for a producer, outlined additional requirements for an open position in its Hong Kong operation. These included good computer skills, the ability to handle multiple tasks at the same time, and the potential for supervising other members of the production team.

The reference to other team members highlights a key to success, which is a television producer's ability to work with others, both in a managerial and in a collaborative role. Marvin Konveleski, a television producer at Access Communications in Canada, confirms this:

Teamwork is very, very important. You have to allow each member of the team to contribute freely and to provide an atmosphere where creativity can come forward in its best and strongest. . . . It also takes a lot of knowing individuals and a lot of give and take compromise—negotiation. Being aware that your answers are not the only answers, the only way of doing it. Knowing that we're all working towards the same goal—that it's the best television product that we can produce with the resources we have available.[15]

Television producer positions are not just limited to broadcast facilities. Many large companies have studios that rival those of television stations in small to midsize cities. Such businesses need producers to create commercials, educational videos, and programs on events of special interest to employees, such as a groundbreaking ceremony for a new corporate building or the introduction of a new company-wide procedure. In some cases, the producer may also function as a director for a given project.

Lorne Michaels (left) talks to Mick Jagger on the set of Saturday Night Live. *As producer of a television show Michaels has many jobs to do, including coordinating the activities of the actors, guest stars, directors, and writers.*

Regardless of where the producer works, the work is seldom routine or dull. What is expected of a television producer is described on the *Princeton Review* Web site:

Television producers make sure that television shows run smoothly in all details, and take responsibility for everything from coordinating writers and performers/correspondents right down to overseeing the fact-checking of credit names and titles. "You're always scrambling up to air time, checking information, and making sure [the show] goes right," wrote one producer. Having complete responsibility for all facets of on-air production can be a very stressful job, and the successful TV producer has to be tightly organized, able to communicate clearly and succinctly with everyone on and off the set, from actors to directors to writers to technical crew, and they must have a gift for thinking on their feet, ready to come up with creative ideas fast under extraordinary time pressure.[16]

Producers typically work long hours—sometimes fourteen hours a day. Television producer Elizabeth Wilson loves her career, but she also knows about its downside:

I work hard but receive little recognition for the success of a show. It's stressful and hectic—I never get enough sleep! Sometimes I feel like a juggler! Even though I like what I do, it's hard to keep all the balls in the air every day. And if I drop one, I know there's someone waiting in the wings—

Paul Slavin (left), executive producer of ABC's World News Tonight, *meets with anchor Peter Jennings.*

What Producers Would Like to Change

Although the majority of producers would not change their job for any other, some say they would change one thing: the constant need to educate a few of their clients on the worth of the process. While many customers understand and appreciate what goes into translating an idea into a finished product, there are those who assume that producers can do what they do effortlessly and quickly. When the client has that misconception, producers feel that there is not a proper degree of respect for the course of action to be followed. A certain progression must happen between the first meeting and the finished program to ensure success. Even though time is money to both the client and the producer, putting together a quality production requires carefully defined steps. When allowance is made for investing the proper time and resources, the result is a better product and a satisfied customer.

or on my own staff—ready to take my job and try to do it better.[17]

The compensation for the stress and long hours comes in the form of moments of high excitement and job satisfaction. Producers take on a project, analyze it, implement it, and enjoy seeing all the elements come together. There is a great deal of personal satisfaction when a production comes to a successful conclusion.

Producers ultimately take credit for a successful broadcast but also have to take the blame for anything that goes wrong on their watch. Yet few people outside of the cast and crew are aware of the motivating force a producer contributes. As one fifteen-year veteran, quoted in the *Princeton Review* article, states, "Only other producers can tell a really well-produced show. You never get any fan-mail." Another producer adds, "It's not as glamorous as it seems on television."[18] He illustrates his point by saying that even the smallest detail must be checked and rechecked before a show goes on the air. A good producer should have enough of an ego to make important decisions and defend them, but he or she should not be afraid of drudge work. For example, even writing copy for an advertisement at the last minute may be a part of the television producer's job. Most producers rise in the ranks from production assistant positions, so they know what it takes to get a show from concept to broadcast.

Education Is a Must

Moving from concept to finished show requires diverse skills in a producer. For this reason, anyone pursuing production as a career soon discovers that there is no such thing as too much education. Again, the competition for the relatively few openings means that those who have not been to college are quickly eliminated.

For those interested in television news production, college course work should include English, journalism, history, political science, meteorology, and American studies. Classes in other areas, such as drama or business, are helpful for those who wish to work in television series production.

Selecting a college that offers the chance to work in a hands-on studio is a must. During lab courses, the student may have the opportunity to produce and direct and also work audio and video control boards, operate a camera, prepare scripts, and even perform before the camera. Although some of these opportunities present themselves later during an internship, the laboratory experience can help the aspiring producer gain access to an internship in the first place.

Internships, even those that are unpaid, are heavily sought after because they provide a big advantage in securing that first paid job in television. Interns get the chance to demonstrate the ability to follow orders, complete tasks, and show initiative by seeking out extra assignments. The savvy intern will make an effort to spend time with producers, directors, and production assistants. Many interns have smoothed their path to a full-time job by getting to know the people who can influence those doing the hiring.

Internships during college offer plenty of rewards, but there is hardly such a thing as starting too early as a producer. A *Hobsons College View* article on the position of television producer states, "There's no substitute for experience, so taking part in high school plays or community theater can be done even during high school. In addition, it is more helpful to the aspiring producer to take advantage of any shadowing or volunteer experiences available at the local television station."[19]

High school and college students can also gain skills and knowledge by working with cable television providers. Most cable television providers offer one or two public access channels, and these channels are usually desperately in need of programming. The ambitious student can help produce programs for these channels, gaining valuable experience in the process.

Learning on the Job

Of course, the point of all the course work and an internship is to prepare for that first job. Competition for entry-level positions is intense, so many aspiring producers take any available job, even if it is in another aspect of the television industry. Doing this

This intern with ESPN demonstrates some of the equipment he works with during his stint as a production assistant.

makes it possible to step into a more directly related assignment, such as that of production assistant, when one opens. Such a position, at least, offers the chance to demonstrate an ability to juggle multiple tasks under stressful circumstances. Still, the duties of a production assistant may be as mundane as proofreading scripts for typos and making lunch reservations for superiors and their guests.

Once a production assistant establishes a willingness to work hard and learn, the responsibilities may be increased to include researching material, arranging and coordinating the details (props, lodging for the crew, catering, and so on) associated with a particular production, and may even involve some writing and directing. Each of these duties adds to the assistant's understanding of the various functions he or she will manage and coordinate as a producer.

Working as a Television Producer

Eventually, the fortunate production assistant lands a position as a producer. By this time, he or she must have learned how to handle almost any task. Producers may screen and hire actors in the morning and do budgets in the afternoon. They may spend one day negotiating contracts with artistic and design personnel and the next day in a remote shooting locale. They spend many hours ensuring that the writers, actors, and production staffs are doing their jobs and that the costs of a production stay within budget.

A producer, therefore, must be adaptable. Producer Konveleski describes other elements of his career that require him to constantly educate himself on technical changes:

> It is very important to be able to adapt in my job and my profession. First of all, there is the technology. The technology is always changing whether it's graphics, whether it's the use of particular hardware (cameras, studio) or whether it's techniques or production tools that come across. So we have to always constantly be aware of what's coming up and trying to reach for that.[20]

Dave Hackel, executive producer of the TV series *Becker*, points out that a producer may also have to fill in for others when problems arise:

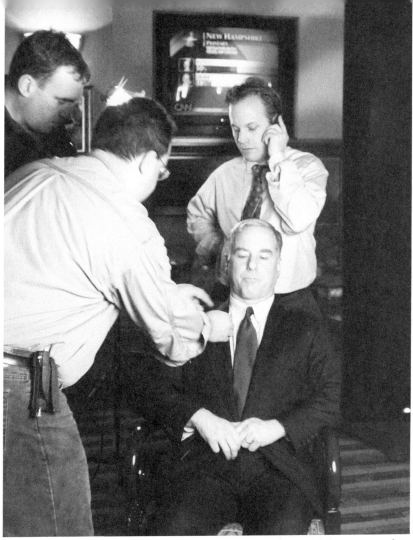

A producer (left) attaches a microphone to presidential candidate Howard Dean before a 2004 interview. Producers often offer their help on set.

When extra help is needed on the set, producers have been known to jump in and operate whatever equipment is necessary. This job entails deft handling of a plethora of daily crises—a camera breaks, bad weather delays filming, a star walks off the set. Even as they are handling all this, producers must simultaneously look ahead to the future, reading hundreds of manuscripts, seeing new films, and maintaining contacts with literary agents and publishers in search of the next big project.[21]

As varied as a producer's tasks may be, there are routines associated with the job. For example, a typical day for a producer assigned to a particular program begins with a meeting with the production staff, consisting of one or more production assistants, the director, and the writers. The discussions will center on coordinating aspects of a production such as audio and camera work, music, timing, writing, and staging. Completed scripts will be reviewed for possible artistic or technical editing, and outlines for new scripts will be distributed to assigned writers. Other issues discussed may concern management policies, production schedules, and budgets for the production.

After dismissing all but the writer and the director, the meeting will be joined by one or more engineers and someone from the set department. The producer will review the scenes to establish camera angles, special effects, scenery or set design, and audio and lighting needs. The producer will also arrange rehearsal times, distribute scripts, book rehearsal facilities, and notify the cast members.

If a rehearsal is part of the day's activities, the producer will attend. He or she will time scenes and calculate programming timing with commercial inserts. During rehearsal, the producer may also select scenes to be taped and used for promoting the show. If the day's work involves the actual live broadcast or taping of the production, then the producer may remain near the director to assist or make last-minute decisions on how to handle any unexpected problems that may arise, such as technical failures or personnel problems.

The producer's work usually includes completing reports on the day's activities and recording all operating costs that have been incurred. Among the duties to be sandwiched in between others are reviewing recordings or rehearsals to make sure work meets production standards, sitting in on postproduction editing of taped programs, and planning out the next day, the next week, and beyond in the continuous cycle of producing content for the voracious appetite of the television audience.

Earnings and Job Opportunities

Someone who can successfully juggle these diverse responsibilities earns, on average, a salary of $46,240 in midsize markets. Yet the salary range is wide, with the lowest 10 percent of producers earning less than $23,300 per year and the highest 10 percent

Producer Levels

A number of individuals handle tasks that make it possible for producers to do their jobs. Production assistants hold entry-level jobs, in which they gain knowledge in many technical, personal, and artistic areas of production. They help the producer in numerous production activities, but especially with administrative tasks. They manage mail, schedule actors, take notes, and make travel arrangements for the producer. Office production assistants do the grunt work for the office production coordinators or the production manager, and set production assistants do the same for assistant directors.

Associate producers handle details for executive producers. They assist the producer with finances or administration and help producers who are collaborating with one another to coordinate, write, and edit productions. Associate producers can specialize in casting, props, and wardrobes. Those in news production assist in setting up stories, gather information and sound bites, and help producers in the control room to execute newscasts.

Executive producers are the top dogs in the producing world. They keep an eye on the big picture, working with long-range planning and budgets, television ratings, and corporate policies. They rarely handle the details of day-to-day production. Instead, they leave this to producers working under them.

As associate producer at Spanish-language network Univision, Beatriz Gomez provides administrative support to the network's executive producer.

earning more than $119,760. Many producers do not earn a fixed wage; instead, they receive a percentage of the income generated by the sales of their productions. This is especially true of series, sports, and special-events programs.

According to the U.S. Department of Labor's Bureau of Labor Statistics, the job outlook for producers should continue to increase: "Employment for producers is expected to grow about as fast (10–20 percent) as the average for all occupations through 2012. Although a growing number of people will aspire to enter these professions, many will leave the field early because the work—when it is available—is hard, the hours are long, and the pay is low."[22]

This means that openings for persons willing to accept the challenges will continue to be available. In addition, the number of cable and satellite channels continues to increase, creating more demand for producers. Competition for jobs as producers will nevertheless be keen because this occupation attracts so many people who regard it as glamorous.

Beyond the glamorous aspects of the work, successful producers find that the real reward is knowing they have made a customer happy. Konveleski says:

> The most satisfying part of my job is the twinkle in the eyes of my clients at the end of production when they've seen the work and they've accomplished it. As a television producer for a cable company, my job is very unique in that I'm dealing with clients who are not familiar with television at all. In fact, they are awed by it. They are very self-conscious and don't know what the heck it is that they're gonna be experiencing when they come in. So when they come in and we walk through the procedure and they learn about television and they end up doing things and they see their dreams, their creative blurb on the screen and they walk away happy with that (sometimes ecstatic with that)—that's the most satisfying thing in the world. I've been able to follow through with them and give them that experience, that delight of creating television, communicating their message in that medium and satisfying their needs.[23]

Chapter 4

Broadcast Engineer

Regardless of the time, effort, and money spent on producing great programming, nothing leaves the television station without the skills of the broadcast engineers. These technical professionals go by a number of different titles, as this job description by the U.S. government's Bureau of Labor Statistics indicates: "Broadcast (engineers) perform a variety of duties in small stations. In large stations and at the networks, technicians are more specialized, although job assignments may change from day to day. The terms operator, engineer, and technician often are used interchangeably to describe these jobs."[24]

According to author Jeanne Nagle, who makes a study of careers, the television technician must be both mentally and physically agile. She explains:

> Broadcast technicians have to be good at working with their hands. They also have to be good at math and science to understand how the machinery they use works and how to get the most out of it. With all the new electronic equipment and the refinements made to the machines they already operate, broadcast and sound technicians need to keep up with current technology.[25]

A broad range of skills is often demanded. Sometimes, engineers must work on location, away from access to other staff members and well-equipped workshops. In such situations they often are called on to be the jacks-of-all-trades, serving as electricians, mechanics, designers, and even inventors in order to keep all the complex systems working.

*An engineer broadcasts videotape of former president Bill Clinton.
Broadcast engineers oversee all of the studio's complex systems.*

Furthermore, the U.S. Department of Labor notes, "All (television) station operations must comply with Federal Communication (FCC) regulations with regard to the quality of the programming and transmitted signal and other applicable local, state, and federal laws. Therefore, a thorough knowledge of FCC regulations is a prerequisite."[26] Meeting those standards is a primary concern of the engineers. As broadcasting technology develops, engineers are also called on to design facility changes to accommodate new or updated equipment, evaluate costs and specifications, and then install new equipment.

In the studio, engineers tend to specialize in either audio or video, but all are charged with setting up, operating, and maintaining a wide variety of electrical and electronic systems involved in creating and broadcasting television programming. In smaller markets, they also set up and control fixed and portable lighting instruments. Larger unionized stations and companies assign technicians to specific tasks, such as lighting and set management.

As owner of his own video production company, Paul Thorman wears many hats. Through his previous experience in broadcasting, he has learned the technical side of television, which he describes in a telephone interview:

> The duties expected of an engineer are the maintenance, repair, and operation of video switchers and special effects generators, audio mixing consoles and related audio source equipment, recording machines, portable and studio cameras, teleprompters and titling systems, lighting instruments, transmitters, and all of the video and audio monitors and monitoring instruments that make up a broadcast or production house facility.[27]

Twenty-first-century engineers have had to learn new technologies. A typical job listing posted on one Web site describes an engineering position available: "Requires knowledge of Windows NT, networking hardware, Internet communications protocols, as well as experience with Web design and development in HTML." The listing also suggests: "Knowledge of satellite, microwave, and fiber optic distribution would be beneficial."[28] The modern broadcast engineer must also be familiar with the operation of mobile electronic newsgathering (ENG) vans, satellite uplinks and downlinks, microwave transmission, and mobile Electronic News Gathering (ENG) and Electronic Field Production (EFP) units for live and recorded feeds outside of the studio.

The U.S. Department of Labor notes:

> The transition to digital recording, editing, and broadcasting has greatly changed the work of broadcast and sound engineering technicians and radio operators. Software on desktop computers has replaced specialized electronic equipment in many recording and editing functions. Most radio and television stations have replaced video and audio tapes with computer hard drives and other computer data storage systems. Computer networks linked to the specialized equipment dominate modern broadcasting.

This transition has forced technicians to learn computer networking and software skills.[29]

With the advent of digital equipment to replace outdated analog systems, modern engineers have the added requirement to be familiar with computers, software, and, in some cases, with basic computer programming languages. A listing of engineering positions posted online by the Society of Broadcast Engineers illustrates the additional computer skills sought by today's television industry:

Broadcast Engineer is needed in Rock Island, Illinois. Must be familiar with news operations, system integration, and computer installation and repair.

Maintenance Engineer is needed in Tulsa, Oklahoma. Skills: Knowledge of digital theory, microprocessor, computer operations, computer operating systems, as well as general solid-state electronics.

Computers in Television

Particularly since the 1990s, computers have become an integral part of everyday life, and that includes the broadcast industry. As computers are being used extensively for control and graphics, there is an increasing need for engineers who are computer-support specialists. This opens the door for computer-savvy individuals who want to be a part of the television industry. Television stations and video production houses have converted, for the most part, to digital technology, and all will be required to do so over the next few years. The operations based on computers include editing systems, special effects, weather graphics, titling generators, teleprompters, and automated control systems. Almost every computer encounters a problem occasionally, and the explosion of computer use has created a high demand for specialists to provide software programming as well as day-to-day administration, maintenance, and support of computer systems and networks.

An engineer works on a live webcast of the 2000 Democratic convention.
Because television stations routinely broadcast over the Internet, engineers
must be very computer literate.

> Chief Engineer is needed in Rock Island, Illinois. This posi-
> tion requires studio, transmitter, live/remote, and computer
> maintenance experience.[30]

As the repeated reference suggests, engineers must be computer literate. Because television stations have begun to broadcast over the Internet, engineers are expected to coordinate all
aspects of live and on-demand Internet broadcasts and to possess
the knowledge needed to aid in the production of audio and
video for any or all of the major multimedia platforms: Windows
Media, QuickTime, and Real.

Educational Requirements

The job market, then, determines who can be a broadcast engineer. As recently as 1995, broadcast technicians were required
by the Federal Communications Commission (FCC) to be
licensed, which required taking courses and banks of tests. The
Telecommunications Act of 1996 eliminated this requirement. As
Nagle points out, however, there are still advantages to studying

as though one were pursuing a license: "While the FCC no longer requires that broadcast technicians be licensed, certification is like a seal of approval that tells prospective employers that you are competent and knowledgeable. In addition to trade schools, associations such as a society or broadcast engineer's offer certification to those who know their craft, and can pass a written exam."[31]

The best way to obtain the training for a broadcast and sound engineering technician job is to attend technical school, community college, or four-year college courses in electronics, computer networking, and broadcast technology. Few high schools are geared to provide the training needed to operate modern television equipment. There are many formulas, rules, and laws of physics involved in working in these career positions, and a good understanding of the principles is essential.

It is especially important that aspiring engineers attend an institution that provides access to a well-equipped studio where they can operate complex switchers, mixing boards, cameras, and other highly technical equipment. The Department of Labor notes that advancement in the engineering field requires more than a high school diploma: "Experienced technicians can become supervisory technicians or chief engineers. A college degree in engineering is needed in order to become chief engineer at a large television station."[32]

As with any skilled professional career, part of an our engineer's training should be participation in related intern programs. Vernon Stone, a professor at University of Missouri, stresses the importance of becoming an intern. He explains his reasoning: "Internships pay off at hiring time. Interns are favored applicants in the growing competition for jobs. In both television and radio, former interns at the same station account for at least one of every six hires. My 1991 survey found that for every three TV interns on duty during a 12-month period, one who had served there before was being hired."[33]

A Typical Day for a Broadcast Engineer

One advantage to an internship is that a newly hired technician will already have a good understanding of the daily routines. Technicians at large stations and networks usually work a forty-hour week under great pressure to meet broadcast deadlines, and they may occasionally work overtime. Technicians at small stations routinely work more than forty hours a week. Evening, weekend, and holiday work is common since most stations are on the air eighteen to twenty-four hours a day, seven days a week. In addition, if a problem arises, a technician who is not on duty may still be called in to assist in correcting any situation that could interfere with the station's ability to broadcast. Such an emergency could involve transmitter failure, which would require the engineer to make repairs, or a power outage, which would require manual switching to backup generators.

Whether they are handling an emergency or are going about their routine duties, broadcast engineers generally work indoors where temperature and humidity are carefully controlled. However, those who handle and operate the equipment used to broadcast news and other programs from locations outside the studio may work outdoors in all types of weather. In addition, technicians do maintenance that may involve climbing poles or

Engineer Specialists

Broadcast technicians in small television stations must perform a variety of duties. In large stations and at the networks, technicians are more specialized, although job assignments may change from day to day. Transmitter operators monitor and log outgoing signals and operate transmitters. Maintenance technicians set up, adjust, service, and repair electronic broadcasting equipment. Audio control engineers regulate sound pickup, transmission, and switching, and video control engineers regulate the quality, brightness, and contrast of television pictures. Recording engineers operate and maintain video and sound recording equipment. Technicians operate equipment designed to produce special effects, such as the illusions of a bolt of lightning or a police siren. Field technicians set up and operate portable field transmission equipment outside the studio. Chief engineers supervise all the technicians who operate and maintain broadcasting equipment.

antenna towers. Most jobs are not physically demanding, although setting up equipment can involve heavy lifting.

On a typical day, a broadcast engineer is required to use highly specialized equipment to regulate the signal strength, clarity, and range of sounds and colors of a television broadcast. An engineer may also maintain and repair the equipment that will be used, so a large portion of an engineer's work takes place before and after a broadcast.

Although all broadcast engineers take the same basic courses to prepare for their career and can therefore fulfill all basic requirements, such as making simple repairs and adjustments to equipment, most specialize in one aspect of producing what viewers finally see on their television sets. Author Shonan Noronha describes the different types of broadcast technicians in his textbook *Opportunities in Television and Video Careers:*

Most broadcast engineers specialize in a particular aspect of production. This audio engineer is performing a sound check before a presidential debate.

Video technicians set up and operate the video equipment, switchers, cameras, video monitors, digital and/or analog video recording equipment, and other video devices such as special effects generators and titling systems.

Video control engineers, on the other hand, are often in a room to themselves to monitor and adjust the quality of the pictures coming from cameras and other video sources in order to assure that the video portion of the broadcast meets FCC requirements.

Audio technicians set up and operate audio equipment, including mixing consoles, microphones, sound speakers, audio recording equipment, and all of the audio monitoring devices that keep volume levels and quality within acceptable broadcast ranges.

Videotape engineers work with prerecorded portions of a show. They operate the videotape recording and playback units so that taped interviews and stories can be run when the program's director calls for them during a live broadcast. They are also responsible for making sure commercials are cued, ready to be aired at the scheduled time.[34]

Broadcast engineers who work in the studio need to be on the ball at all times during the telecast. Part of their job involves juggling input from a number of different sources. They may be working with multiple cameras in the studio, or they may have to cut to a live broadcast and then cut in a taped segment—all on cue and at very specific times.

Once a program is under way, the engineers work according to the program director's instructions. In order to produce a technically successful show, each of the various engineers involved must have a sense of "the big picture" and be able to cooperate seamlessly with each other. When the production—whether live or recorded—is over, the engineer's work is not finished. Any malfunctioning equipment must be tagged for repair, logs must be filled out, and the studio and equipment might need to be restored to their original settings for the next program scheduled for production there. In addition, the director and/or producer may call a meeting with the staff to discuss the day's work and to list problem areas and needed changes for future productions.

Engineer Earnings

The pay broadcast engineers earn for their many diverse duties varies widely. Commercial television stations—those operated for profit—usually pay more than public broadcasting stations, which are usually supported by grants and donations. Moreover, stations in large markets pay more than those in small markets. According to the U.S. Department of Labor, "Median annual earnings of broadcast technicians in 2002 were $27,760. The middle 50 percent earned between $18,860 and $45,200. The lowest 10 percent earned less than $14,600, and the highest 10 percent earned more than $65,970."[35]

Offering the potential for even higher income is freelance work—that is, temporary assignments with whoever needs a technician for a particular project. Freelance sound and lighting technicians get paid by the day. Depending on their experience, they make three to four hundred dollars for ten to twelve hours a day. However, a freelancer may have to supply his or her own equipment, which is very expensive. In addition, freelance work comes with no fringe benefits, such as health insurance.

The Job Outlook

One factor that should lead to higher earnings in the future is growth in demand for technicians and engineers. The phenomenal expansion of the cable television industry has contributed to the increase. Furthermore, the growing use of television in industry, government, and education means that broadcast television stations are having to compete to hire engineers. Job offers listed on the Internet abound as stations across the country look for help. Most engineers will find security in such a market, and it is normal to find technicians working well past retirement ages at some stations.

Despite the demand for qualified personnel, most jobs for those starting out are in smaller cities and towns. In major metropolitan areas the number of qualified job seekers typically exceeds the number of openings; thus, stations generally hire only highly experienced personnel.

One factor that may limit job growth in television broadcasting is consolidation of ownership of television stations. The Department of Labor notes:

> Changes to Federal Communications Commission (FCC) regulations now under consideration may allow the ownership of as many as eight radio and TV stations in a single metropolitan area. Owners of multiple stations often consolidate many of their operations into a single location, reducing employment because one or a few technicians can provide support to multiple stations.[36]

Why the Switch Is on to Digital Television

The modern broadcast technician is required to be familiar with the concept and operation of digital equipment for television. Much of this is driven by the government's mandate for television broadcasters to be equipped to send and television sets to be able to receive digital signals by 2007. Viewers of digital television now enjoy higher quality audio and video, a huge range of new general and specialty channels, and far more choice and control over what they watch. Digital television has also enabled television broadcasters to deliver a wide range of new services to viewers. Many game and quiz shows now allow viewers to participate in the program through interactive television (iTV). This not only decreases channel surfing by locking the viewer into the channel, but it also can generate significant revenue for the broadcaster by asking viewers to pay a small amount for the privilege of interacting. Live events, such as sports or music, also have been revolutionized by iTV. Viewers now can choose their preferred way of watching a game or concert by selecting alternative video feeds from different cameras or alternative audio streams with perhaps different commentaries to focus on one individual. Whether that concept is good or bad remains to be seen, but digital technology has changed forever the way the television is viewed.

An engineer tests a closed-circuit television system. As the television industry continues to expand, the job outlook for broadcast engineers remains promising.

Economists who follow the television industry say that employment of broadcast and sound engineering technicians in the cable and pay television portion of the broadcasting industry should grow as the range of services is expanded to provide such products as cable Internet access and video on demand.

Contributing to the demand for broadcast engineers is the growth in other industries that require knowledge of electronics, such as the computer industry. As the use of electronic controls in manufacturing of all kinds grows, technicians who can maintain and repair this new equipment will be needed as well, possibly drawing people away from broadcasting.

Even as competition for their services improves their earnings potential, broadcast engineers find that more is required of them. The quality of video and audio signals transmitted by a station depends on the work of its engineering and technical staff. Also of great importance is the performance and reliability of professional video equipment used in production or postproduction facilities and in corporate video departments. Shonan Noronha follows the trends in television and reports, "As the level of sophistication of equipment constantly increases, so do the demands that the technicians and engineers upgrade their skills and become proficient in handling new technology."[37]

FCC chairman Michael K. Powell challenged the television industry to react quickly to the FCC requirement to enhance up to 50 percent of their schedules with value-added digital programming, which will benefit viewers, as Powell noted, "with super sharp television pictures and even more entertainment and educational choices."[38] This places a premium on the skills of technicians and engineers who are well versed in these new technologies.

Job Mobility

One way of improving one's earnings is through a lateral move— keeping the same job title but moving from a small station to a larger one or from a small market to a larger one. In addition, vertical job mobility is a common way to advance. For example, an engineering technician with several years of experience in a station may get promoted to the position of senior engineer and eventually into management as the engineering supervisor.

Few jobs offer the variety to be found in working as a broadcast technician. In addition to the fulfillment of being able to operate complex audio and video equipment, there is the creative satisfaction of blending multiple sources of image and sound to produce programs that inform, entertain, or instruct audiences. The combination of opportunities for advancement in position and income, and the glamour of television, offer much to the person with the natural talent and inclination for a career in a technical field.

Chapter 5

Creative Writer

The term *creative writer* covers a number of different categories. Stations in major markets employ staff writers who create promotional pieces for upcoming programs, write copy for factual inserts for sporting events, and generate public relations spots. Copywriters specialize in creating advertising copy to sell products and services. Screenwriters produce original scripts for features, documentaries, and series programming, and they are responsible for much of the content seen on the television screen.

News writers prepare content for newscasts by acquiring the details and facts from Reuters, the Associated Press, and other major news organizations and assemble them into stories of the length and style used by their particular television station. Editors review, edit, and rewrite the work of the different creative writers and may do some of the writing themselves.

The U.S. Bureau of Labor Statistics' *Occupational Outlook Handbook* for writers and editors describes the nature of the work:

> Writers, especially of nonfiction, are expected to establish their credibility with producers and viewers through strong research and the use of appropriate sources and citations. Sustaining high ethical standards and meeting publication deadlines are essential. Such writers, who are often freelancers hired and paid by the job, either propose a topic or are assigned one by the producer or a commercial client. They gather information about the topic through personal observation, library and Internet research, and interviews.[39]

Only after completing their research do most writers sit down at the computer and actually compose the first draft of a script. This is especially true of nonfiction content like documentaries. Writers revise or rewrite a piece many times, searching for the best organization or the right phrasing.

Writing is hard work. Speak with any novelist, reporter, or screenwriter and the same comments will be heard. Writing can be the best job in the world, and the worst. The stress of dead-lines, the long hours of researching and revising, and the stacks of rejection slips can wear away at all but the most dedicated. Add to that the comparatively low pay—except for the few writers at the top—and the dreaded computer crash that sends hours of work into infinity.

Getting That First Job

Despite the difficulties, those same writers will likely be the first to encourage a dedicated and talented person to never give up his

Screenwriters take part in an industry discussion panel. Screenwriters produce the scripts for almost all television programming.

A Writer's View of Television Screenwriting

In Richard Toscan's online article entitled "Writing for Television," Steven Bochco, the prolific television screenwriter of such hit series as Ironside, NYPD Blue, Hill Street Blues, Murder One, *and many others, provides an unusual perspective on his successful career. In spite of huge paydays, he has this to say about writing for television:*

The tube is death on writers. Especially television series work. It rots talent at an astounding rate—or at least the kind of talent playwrights need. Yes, mostly it's brainless stuff, but the real culprit is the demand for speed and repetition. You're writing as part of a team—often with five or six other writers. And you're laboring within strict formulas for the show's characters and plots. It's like making Pintos at the Ford plant: you stamp out the body [with lots of help] and somebody else puts in the headlight. And you're doing it fast: 14 days is luxury for about 45 pages of dialogue.

If you leap at television series work, you'll make a ton of money—if the series is a hit and gets that 5-year run. And even if you don't get that magic 5-year run, you'll still make a quarter-ton. If you're like most, you'll figure then maybe you can afford to write plays.

Screenwriter Steven Bochco (second from left) celebrates the two hundredth episode of NYPD Blue, *one of several successful shows he helped bring to life.*

or her dream and to keep writing in hopes of landing that first assignment. To get a job, the fledgling writer must behave as though he or she already has the job. The most common entry into a television writing career is to submit two or more completely scripted episodes for an established series. In other words, show producers look for sample episodes that are written as if the writer were already on staff. Writers pursuing the opportunity to script a series will often record on tape or DVD any show of interest. Having the capability to view the content a number of times permits the writer to study characters, sets, speech and movement patterns, and to outline the acts within the program. If the show's producers feel that the script has an original plot and has accurately captured the show's characters and voice, then the writer may be invited to interview for a position on the show's staff. An example would be the recent popular series *Friends*.

The characters were well established, as were the themes, the sets, and the type of writing that was desired. A search of the Internet under the term *sample scripts* or under the name of a particular program can often provide a complete script for a particular episode. Using that as a template, a talented, educated, and experienced writer can configure original ideas to match the broad, established outline of the series.

There are rare exceptions to this rule. One writer of more than five hundred hours of network television, Larry Brody, broke into his career not by submitting episodes for an existing series but by showing his own original material. While a student at Northwestern University, Brody wrote a number of scripts, which he presented to an agent who was having his eyes examined at the office of Brody's fiancée's father, an optometrist. He describes the encounter: "Sitting there with his pupils dilated while my future father-in-law told him what a great writer I was, the poor guy had no choice but to agree to talk to me and read what I had. He did, however, have a choice about whether or not to like what he saw, and, fortunately, he liked it a lot."[10]

Brody goes on to note that he submitted a number of stories at once, establishing his willingness to work hard. James A. Mac Eachern is a freelance screenwriter who knows that behind the glamour of receiving awards from such organizations as the Writers Guild, the American Film Institute, or Mystery Writers, there is a lot of hard work: "Screenwriting is an art, a craft, and the business, and unless you are committed to learning, practicing, and perfecting the skills necessary to write a good script, you will never rise above the fierce competition, and claim potentially huge awards of a major writer."[41]

As hard as the work can be, only relatively recently have television writers found respect for their creativity. Cheryl Harris, in her online article "Writer in Television" explains how Hollywood's influence downplayed the importance of the television writer:

> With the television industry's move to Hollywood [from New York] in the 1950s, and its increasing reliance on filmed, formulaic, studio factory productions, writers were often reduced to "hack" status, churning out familiar material that was almost interchangeable across genres. This week's western could be reformatted for next week's crime drama. This view oversimplifies, of course, and ignores extraordinary work in television series such as [the early 1960s series] Naked City, The Defenders, Route 66 and others. However, it does capture conventional assumptions and expectations.[42]

As audiences became more sophisticated, however, such carbon-copy material was no longer acceptable, and writers gained stature. Gradually, their voices and opinions were heard by studio executives. Now, writers are often able to oversee series development and production and create new programs. Their skills are highly valued and, for the very successful few, extremely highly rewarded. Harris goes on to describe the impact that a few progressive individuals have had in elevating the writer's position in the television industry:

> Television authors such as Dennis Potter and Lynda La Plante have offered audiences outstanding, often formally challenging work for this medium. Because of their work . . . television writing is now perhaps recognized as a truly legitimate form of creativity, and has taken its place alongside the novel, the stage play, and the film screenplay as one of the most central expressive forms of the age.[43]

Today, writers are recognized for their contributions to the success of a show. These writers for As The World Turns *are showing off their Emmy awards in 2004.*

Nevertheless, the role of the writer is affected by many other issues, and despite new respect and prominence, the writer's position remains complex and often conflicted within the television industry. The Writers Guild of America and comparable organizations around the world continue to negotiate for greater artistic control as well as better pay and benefits for writers. There has been improvement at least for writers in television dramatic series. These series are entirely dependent on the skills of the writer, director, and actor, with the writer often being the most important. Television producer Stephen Smallwood illustrates that point with his description of how he divides his time between the three types of artists:

> If you want to analyze which is the most important, I think you would be very hard pushed to say it. All I can say to you is, as a producer I spend about 65 to 70 percent of my time working with the writers. And therefore from my perspective as a TV producer, the writing is the most difficult bit and the most important bit. You can make a very very bad television series out of bad scripts and you can make a very very good television series out of very good scripts but you

The Process of Writing a Television Series

In an interview with Jenna Glatzer of the Absolute Write Web site, Tom Lynch, the creator and writer of numerous hit programs for kids of all ages for more than twenty years, was asked what a series writer goes through after getting an assignment. He describes the process:

I can only tell you about my shows. It begins with the writers pitching ideas to the producers and me. We then choose the ones we like and develop premises for each one. Next, we get the network executives to approve them.

When they are approved, we go to "the board," where we break the story into an outline. This can take anywhere from a day to a week, a month or longer. In one case, it took a full year and a half to develop an episode on HIV [the human immunodeficiency virus] for *Scout's Safari*.

Once I approve the story outline, it goes to the network executives to provide notes. We will discuss the notes and either go to script or abandon the story. If it goes to script, the writer goes off and writes. The writer will turn in the draft, the producers and I will read it and give notes. The notes will be addressed and then go to network. After we get the network notes, we all get in a room and table the script, where we cut the fat, punching jokes all the way until we film.

can't make a very good television series out of bad scripts and that is the key. If you got the scripts right you have a fighting chance of making a good television series and then the skill is to get the best directors and the best actors. Script from my point of perspective is the most important thing and therefore the selection of writers is vitally important.[44]

Beyond looking for an ability to conform to a series' requirements, potential employers look for other qualities in a writer. Emmy winner Tom Lynch, who is a producer/writer for several NBC series for kids, defines what qualities he seeks in a writer:

For starters, the craft itself is very important. I've actually run across writers who can't complete a script and that's not acceptable. Imagination as well as a fresh perspective on things is also very important. I love being in a room full of writers who come up with ideas that I haven't heard or done before . . . but they have to be grounded in reality, too! They also need to be *fun*. (I am not a fan of the pain style of writing or attitude in general.) If I'm going to be with this writer for six months in a highly stressful situation (and every one of my TV series projects falls into this category), then I want to be able to enjoy the collaboration.[45]

In an interview, Lynch delved into his own experience as a hopeful screenwriter to offer this advice to other aspiring writers: "Write like someone is going to watch and listen. It is a craft, so practice it. Meanwhile, don't get discouraged. I've outlasted many network executives who have thought my ideas weren't worthy. In fact, my shows are still on the air while they are out looking for new jobs!"[46]

Education and Internships

Although those in a position to hire writers look first at the samples the applicant submits, there are also basic qualifications to be met. A college degree generally is required for a position as a writer. While some employers look for a broad liberal arts background, most prefer to hire someone with a degree in communications, journalism, or English. For those who wish to specialize in a particular area, such as fashion, business, or legal issues, additional background in the chosen field is expected. Knowledge of a second language is helpful for some positions. Successful writers also advise taking courses that involve writing in a number of genres, including short stories, poetry, and essays. These writers also say that courses requiring one completed work every week are good preparation for the rigid deadlines that a writer faces under actual working conditions.

Many colleges offer opportunities for students to be involved in stage plays and programs produced by the school's television station. Experienced writers say that taking part in plays or broadcasts this way helped them understand the process of moving from written words to the final production.

Before working on television and movies, screenwriter Alan Ball worked as a playwright in New York.

As in most other careers in television, the aspiring writer should seek out internships. Not only can an internship provide greater understanding of the "real" world of television, but such a position offers a chance to acquire those all-important contacts that can lead to employment in the future. In the article "How to Be a TV Writer," the NBC Career Opportunities Web site offers suggestions for intern positions that can open doors for graduates:

> There are many ways to get your foot in the door. Some of the more common ways include: Becoming a reader (a person who evaluates and writes synopses of scripts for a literary production company or a network), being a production assistant, being a writer's assistant, or being an assistant to a producer. Most of these jobs are at the production level and the production companies should be contacted directly for more information. Writer training programs are another avenue you may want to explore.[47]

Workshops

Indeed, writer training programs, or workshops, can be extremely helpful. They present one with a first opportunity to put one's words in front of a critical audience. Successful writers caution, however, that workshops, particularly scriptwriting workshops, have a tendency over time to become the end rather than the means to an end. The danger is that participants begin to write for their peers. The result can be writing that sounds so standardized that it fails to gain the notice of those who are looking for fresh new talent.

Still, several workshop programs are recommended by NBC, with a few precautions added:

Warner Brothers Workshop; Disney Fellowship, Nickelodeon Fellowship Program, and Writers Guild Training Program. Never stay in any one workshop for more than one year, and never take more than two such prolonged workshops in

Writing for Television

J. Michael Straczynski, a screenwriter for Babylon 5; Murder, She Wrote; *and other programs, is also the author of* The Complete Book of Scriptwriting. *In his discussion on different types of writing, he states:*

Writing for television, is at once the easiest and the most difficult branch of scriptwriting. Easy in that many factors are predetermined: the length to the script, the number of acts, the range of permissible topics and the characters you'll be dealing with. The schematic has already been set down. Your task as a writer is to plug in your own ideas into that context, which for some writers is where the process becomes quite difficult. You are required to work with characters created by someone other than yourself, structure your story around commercials and other artificial timing devices, set aside your ego when the producer says, "Our character there wouldn't do that," and limit yourself in the number of sets and the types of situation you can develop into storylines.

any three-year period. Additionally, be careful in your selection of the workshop, make sure your instructor knows what he is talking about and has real credits. Read the descriptions, and, most important, read between the lines.[48]

A common question beginning writers ask is whether they need an agent to get a writing job. The answer is that, while not impossible, getting a writer job without some type of representation is harder than if one has an agent. Agents, for example, are aware that the staffing season (March through June) is when the bulk of writers get jobs on television shows and therefore contact producers when those all-important individuals are most likely to be interested in reading scripts.

Working Conditions

Once a writer finds a job, working conditions can vary widely. Some writers work in comfortable, private offices; others work in noisy rooms filled with the sound of keyboards and computer printers as well as the voices of other writers tracking down information over the telephone. Most writers will find themselves making at least basic use of technology, regularly using personal computers, desktop or electronic publishing systems, scanners, and other electronic equipment. The search for information sometimes requires that the writer travel to diverse workplaces, such as factories, offices, or laboratories, but many find their material through telephone interviews, at the library, and on the Internet.

The working hours may not be long, but they can be uneven. The U.S. Department of Labor explains some of the conditions that face the writer:

> For some writers, the typical workweek runs 35 to 40 hours. However, writers occasionally work overtime to meet deadlines. Those who prepare morning or weekend broadcasts work some nights and weekends. Freelance writers generally work more flexible hours, but their schedules must conform to the needs of the client. Writers are not immune to many of the deadlines and erratic work hours, often part of the daily routine in these jobs, may cause stress, fatigue, or

The working conditions of screenwriters can vary widely. This writer is lucky enough to work in the comfort of his own private office.

burnout. Changes in technology and electronic communications also affect a writer's work environment. For example, laptops allow writers to work from home or on the road. Writers and editors who use computers for extended periods may experience back pain, eyestrain, or fatigue.[49]

While workers in other careers experience similar conditions, few are exposed to them to the same degree as a writer. As deadlines near, it is not unusual for a writer to work long hours and for days without a break.

The Writer's Prospects

People who choose writing for television as a career generally do so despite the ocassionally difficult working conditions. They are motivated by the joy of creating works that will be seen and heard by others for information and entertainment rather than by the promise of a high income. The Bureau of Labor Statistics reports, "Median annual earnings for salaried (television) writers were $42,790 in 2002. The middle 50 percent earned between $29,150 and $58,930. The lowest 10 percent earned less than $21,320, and the highest 10 percent earned more than $85,140."[50]

Writer Cheryl Harris reinforces the fact that persons seeking a career in writing for television must understand that there are pitfalls. As with any job in the television industry, the attraction of work that seems glamorous must be balanced against the fact that only a small percentage of writers ever realize the dream of wealth: "Although the WGA [Writers Guild of America] sets minimum payments, 70% of television writers earn less than $50,000 a year through their efforts in this field."[51]

In spite of this harsh reality, hundreds of aspiring writers write thousands of new scripts each year, hoping for the chance to write the next huge hit. A recent government report on writing as a career states:

> The outlook for most writing and editing jobs is expected to be competitive, because many people with writing or journalism training are attracted to the occupation. Employment of writers is expected to grow about as fast as the average for all occupations through the year 2012. In addition to job openings created by employment growth, some openings will arise as experienced workers retire, transfer to other occupations, or leave the labor force. Replacement needs are relatively high in this occupation; many freelancers leave because they cannot earn enough money.[52]

Although writing for television can often be tiring and frustrating, and the financial rewards sometimes disappointing, the lure of creative writing still draws people of talent to a career in the television industry. Most writers agree that whether a person is an author seeing his or her book displayed in the window of a bookstore or a television writer seeing his or her creation come to life on the television screen, the feeling of accomplishment when that happens makes all the difficulties seem worthwhile.

Chapter 6

Actor

An actor, also known as talent, is a man, woman, or child whose works express ideas and create images in theater, film, radio, television, and other performing arts media. Actors appear in all types of television programming, and their work may involve a serious or comic role using speech gestures and body movements in their performances. In some cases, they may be required to dance and sing.

Among the skills and abilities of a television actor are the memorizing of lines with accompanying movement and cues and the ability to improvise when there is an unplanned deviation from the script. This is especially true in the case of live programming, when the director cannot halt the production to correct a miscue.

The actor must be able to interpret the script with creativity and imagination to communicate the feelings and ideas the writer and the director intended and to entertain or instruct an audience. Actors must be able to accept constant direction without taking criticism personally. Actors must also be able to imagine an audience's reaction. This is especially true where the audience consists only of the crew.

Much of the content on television involves acting, although this art takes many forms. An actor may host a morning show or a weekly children's program. Others may be hired to do commercials, feature stories, or standup comedy. Because they are seen by a viewing audience, newscasters and weather reporters (meteorologists) are also actors, although they are referred to by the more generic term *talent*. Of course, there are the high-visibility acting jobs—usually found in a continuing drama series or a soap opera.

The dreams of glamour and wealth to be found performing in a popular series or soap opera drive many aspiring actors to look for a career in television. Yet unless a person has either family or professional connections, finds an aggressive agent, or simply

Television actors Sam Waterston and Elisabeth Rohm are very successful in their roles on the hit drama series Law & Order.

happens to be fortunate enough to be in the right place at the right time, the road to success will be long and hard.

Constant Pressure

Even if actors find work in television, they must be able to work under constant pressure. Acting assignments typically are short term—ranging from one day to a few months—and that means actors frequently experience long periods of unemployment between jobs. Many actors face stress from the continual need to find their next job. The uncertain nature of the work results in unpredictable earnings and intense competition for even the lowest-paid jobs. A report by the union that represents television actors, the Screen Actors Guild (SAG), states that more than a third of its members did not receive any earnings under SAG contracts.

Given those facts, the guild suggests that aspiring actors have enough savings to live for two years without any income. In addition, the guild recommends keeping a "day job"—that is, a job unrelated to acting—to keep the bills paid until one lands that first role. That applies to even the most talented performers in a series since anyone can lose a role at the end of the season.

Timothy Fall, a veteran actor in film and television, was warned early on about the struggles of finding work and earning a living as an actor: "When I was a 17-year-old apprentice with a summer theatre company, I was given this advice by the first director I ever worked with: 'If you're thinking of becoming an actor, first, don't do it. Second, if you're too thick-headed to heed the first piece of advice, then be as prepared as you possibly can be.'"[53]

"So You Want to Be an Actor?"

At Linda McAlister's talent agency, she encounters a number of people who ask how they can break into acting. In this excerpt from her online article entitled "So You Want to Be an Actor?," she explains how it is in the real world:

What if someone were to say, "I think I've decided that I'd like to be a surgeon . . . so how do I get started on doing operations?" No matter how many times they've seen *ER*, they'll never be a surgeon unless they have the discipline and desire to work very hard for many years, gaining experience and knowledge. I have to laugh when someone says, "I'd do *anything* if I could be an actor." But when I tell them that it takes hard work, persistent study and often having to take a day job that's well beneath their qualifications simply so they can have a flexible schedule for auditions and shoots, they say, "Oh, I can't do that!" So much for "I'll do anything."

The acting profession is exactly that—a *profession*—and it should be treated with the respect due any profession. For the most part, acting is an acquired skill that is learned through many years of formal classes, study and experience. In order to be an actor, you have to *absolutely love* acting. Why? Because you'll have to give up almost everything else in your life in order to succeed, and if you don't really love it, you stand a chance of being very unhappy.

For fledging actors who decide to trust their future to an unpredictable combination of talent, training, location, look, energy, attitude, and luck, the simplest procedure is to attend open auditions—known among acting professionals as "cattle calls." The sessions are attended by large numbers of people, so actors must be realists and know that the odds are against their getting the part for which they are auditioning. Withstanding frequent rejections is an element of the acting business.

Especially in the early stages of their careers, actors must rely on attending cattle calls, summoning all of their confidence and acting and speaking skills to convince a producer or director that he or she has found the right person for a given role. However, as an actor's reputation and list of successful roles grows, most rely on agents or managers to find work, negotiate contracts, and plan their careers. In return for this help, the actor pays the agent a percentage of what he or she is paid for acting in the part.

An example of how actors are selected would be the tryouts for a reality series called *The It Factor* and described by the *New York Daily News:* "There are nine slots, with the winners followed around for six months by 'It Factor' camera crews. The slots are filled by casting director Mali Finn after three rounds of auditions."[54] The *Daily News* goes on to note that Finn chooses from among those attending the open auditions and from actors whose names have been put forward by agents.

Despite enormous effort, most actors struggle to find steady work, and only a few ever achieve recognition as stars. Even some well-known, experienced performers may have to settle for supporting roles. Those with lesser credentials work as extras, with no lines to deliver, or settle for cameo appearances, speaking only one or two lines. Some actors do voice-over and narration work for advertisements, animated features, books on tape, and other electronic media. A few also teach the skills they have mastered in high school or university drama departments, acting conservatories, or public programs.

There is no single road to becoming an actor, nor is there a particular age when a television acting career may begin. Depending on the nature of the role, television producers may hire very young children and very senior men and women. With such a wide range of roles available, the prospects would seem to

Huge numbers of Elvis impersonators line up to audition for the role of Elvis Presley in a television mini-series.

be excellent for finding work as an actor. Yet the reality is that the competition for jobs is fierce due to the large number of would-be actors.

Increasing Chances for Success

Given the imbalance between the demand for actors and the supply, luck also plays a role in landing a job. Still, there are characteristics that increase an aspiring actor's chance for success. The U.S. Department of Labor details some of these characteristics, often evidenced by the person's desire to perform:

> Employers (of actors) generally look for people with the creative instincts, innate talent, and intellectual capacity to perform. Actors should possess a passion for performing and enjoy entertaining others. This passion should drive the aspiring actor to take part in plays early in high school and later in college. Dedicated actors often began by working in college radio stations, or perform with local community theater groups. There are hundreds of local

and regional theaters that offer experience that can lead to work in summer stock, on cruise lines, or in theme parks.[55]

Preparing for an acting career does not, however, necessarily involve moving to Los Angeles or New York. An education program based in Virginia points out that "in television, opportunities are concentrated in the network centers of New York and Los Angeles, but cable television services and local television stations around the country employ many actors as well."[56]

In fact, most new actors take advantage of openings at local television stations to get a foothold. Some may eventually move up to "the big time," but the majority will find a more comfortable niche in the less competitive arena of small- to medium-sized communities.

Wherever an actor ends up pursuing his or her profession, certain qualities will help gain the attention of those doing the hiring. The U.S. Department of Labor notes:

Directors and producers look for actors with poise, stage presence, the capability to affect an audience, and the ability to follow direction. Physical appearance, such as possessing the right size, weight, or features, often is the decid-

Young girls audition for a movie role at a casting call. Some actors begin their careers at a very young age.

ing factor in being selected for particular roles. Modeling experience may be helpful in order to understand movement and motivation directions.[57]

To be a success, actors also need the commitment to their craft to deliver flawless performances, often while working under undesirable and unpleasant conditions, including long hours. Schedules can occasionally be irregular. Although live television rarely demands that an actor perform outside of daytime programming hours, rehearsals for an upcoming show may require their attendance after hours. On the other hand, actors working on recorded television programs—especially those shot on location—may have to work in the early morning or late evening hours to tape night scenes or scenes inside public facilities outside of normal business hours. They also need the flexibility to travel if a television program is recorded or produced in locations other than the home studio.

Adding to the challenges is the necessity of handling the unexpected without becoming flustered. The Bureau of Labor Statistics explains that this is particularly true of those who are part of a series: "Actors who perform in a television series often appear on camera with little preparation time, because scripts tend to be revised frequently or even written moments before taping. Those working before a live audience must be able to handle impromptu situations and to calmly ad-lib substitute lines when necessary."[58]

Topping off the list of requirements if one is to succeed as an actor is physical fitness, as explained by the U.S. Bureau of Labor Statistics:

Actors should be in good physical condition and have the necessary stamina and coordination to move about large television studios and lots. They also need to maneuver about complex technical sets while staying in character and projecting their voices audibly. Actors must be fit to endure heat from studio lights and the weight of heavy costumes. Producers and directors ensure the safety of actors by conducting extra rehearsals on the set so that the actors can learn the layout of set pieces and props, by allowing time for warm-ups and stretching exercises to guard against physical and vocal injuries, and by providing an adequate number of breaks to prevent heat exhaustion and dehydration.[59]

Formal Training

Having weighed all the pros and cons of an acting career, anyone choosing to persist must look toward gaining the education needed to make the most of innate talent. While there are instances of persons with little or no formal training having been "discovered" by being in the right place at the right time, those are rare exceptions rather than the rule. Acting is a career with many nuances of speech, emotion, movement, awareness of surroundings, knowledge of makeup and costuming, and familiarity with the craft. Many of the attributes sought by producers and directors, in addition to natural talent, are acquired through formal training and practice.

Formal training can be gained either through an acting conservatory or a university program. As part of their training, most aspiring actors take courses in radio and television broadcasting, communications, film, theater, drama, or dramatic literature while studying for a bachelor's degree. Many continue their academic training and receive a master of fine arts degree. Advanced courses may include courses in foreign languages, dialect, movement, directing, playwriting, and set design as well as intensive acting workshops or mentoring by a drama coach. Courses to help students eliminate regional accents may also be offered.

Internships and Freelancing

In addition to course work, many acting programs offer internships. Through college intern programs, actors-in-training not only gain experience and polish skills, but they also learn the language and unique working conditions found in television. Almost as important are the opportunities such placements offer for getting to know the producers and directors who hire talent.

Internships for would-be actors are also offered by some television stations. However, the hunt for an internship should include contacting independent production companies, which do features, infomercials, and commercials. Wherever they serve, interns must be prepared to do menial tasks. They may find that their job includes fetching coffee, putting coins in an assistant

These aspiring actors obtain formal training by participating in a drama program at a university in Massachusetts.

director's parking meter, or handing facial tissues to an actor working under hot lights.

For the intern, performing such seemingly minor chores is important. Promptly doing what is required without complaint will not go unnoticed by those who hire talent. Further, the opportunity to watch a professional cast and crew at work cannot be duplicated in a college lab. Volunteering for any tasks can add to the knowledge and skills needed for an acting career.

The Internet has become a valuable tool for finding internships for actors. Whereas a few internships are paid, most are not, although there may be other benefits. The following is a recent Actors' Gang Web ad that offers training in place of donated hours:

> If you are interested in the internship program, which requires 10 hours per week of donated time in exchange for Style Workshops and the opportunity to audition, please send a headshot/resume and letter describing why you want to be a part of The Actors' Gang to the attention of Blaire Chandler, Hollywood, CA 90038.[60]

Working as an Actor

Of course, interns get the chance to witness firsthand actors at work. That work takes many forms and requires many talents. For

The Teleprompter

People who work in front of the camera use various prompting methods to aid them in their on-camera delivery. Most prompters (often referred to as teleprompters after the original manufacturer) rely on a reflected image of the words on a mirror in front of the camera lens. The image from the video monitor (displaying the text to be read) is reflected into a half-silvered mirror mounted at a forty-five-degree angle to the lens. The image of the text, as seen by the prompter camera, is electronically reversed left to right so that the mirror image will appear correct.

Since the mirror is only half-silvered, it ends up being a two-way mirror. First, it reflects the image from the video prompter screen, allowing the talent to read the text. Second, being semi-transparent, the mirror allows much of the light from the scene being photographed to pass through its surface and go into the camera lens. When the talent looks at the prompter mirror to read the text, it appears as if they are looking right at the viewer through the camera lens. In order not to give the appearance of constantly staring into the camera lens, most on-camera personalities who use prompters periodically glance at their scripts, especially as a way of emphasizing facts and figures.

Vice Presidential nominee Joseph Lieberman reads a speech on a teleprompter at the 2000 Democratic National Convention.

example, an actor may have to deliver memorized lines as part of making an episode in a sitcom or a dramatic series.

More often, if the actor is a show's host, a newscaster, or any talent who speaks directly toward a camera, he or she depends on a teleprompter, a device that is attached to the camera in front of the lens. The content to be spoken is displayed on an angled glass as a moving body of script, paced to the actor's special requirements. Such technology does not completely eliminate the unexpected. Occasional comments may take place between participants that are spontaneous and unscripted.

Advertisements are more structured than other types of television content and provide less opportunity to deviate from the script. This is because the script has been written and rewritten to achieve the most concentrated persuasion possible in the ten, twenty, or sixty seconds it will appear on screen. The actor will be given specific lines and movements for each scene and take. As a result, such assignments are difficult and exacting. An expensively produced commercial lasting one minute may require an entire day's rehearsal and shooting and can be almost as exhausting for talent as doing a half-hour live show.

Much less exacting are news shows. The talent in these productions follow outlines that also contain cues for moving about the set and short written commentaries or introductions to be delivered for each segment. The greater part of the program, however, is nonscripted patter between members of the cast.

Whether their content is carefully scripted or not, actors generally face predictable workdays. All on-camera talent, from newscasters to actors in dramatic series, must go through makeup. This may consist of simple powders to highlight the desired facial features, or it may consist of an elaborate mask or other appliances like a false nose or ears designed to totally change the actor's appearance to match the role. After makeup comes the wardrobe. Depending on the part the talent plays, the wardrobe may involve the business attire of a news anchor or the clown outfit for the host of a children's show. The actors usually go to the set and do a run-through of the show before the tape recorder is started or the program—if it is live—goes on the air.

Daily programming that takes place on an unchanging set, such as a news show, has lighting that is usually adjusted once and left in place. The actors simply walk onto the set and begin the show. In a dramatic series with changing sets and moods, however, there may be long waiting periods for lighting adjustments, control of background noise, touch-ups of hair and makeup, or modifications of camera angles. Then begins multiple takes as the director reviews each scene to make sure it meets the client's needs.

Actors in live television shows avoid the stopping and starting, but the stress level is much higher; once the on-air light is illuminated there is no stopping. It is the actor's ability to keep the show going that can make or break a career, regardless of a wrong line being spoken, a late entry by another actor, or technical glitches such as a malfunctioning prop or a camera failure.

Financial and Personal Rewards

If a person's desire to act is strong enough to face the hard work and the repeated rejections, then the often-paltry income will not be a deterrent either. The average annual earnings of salaried actors were $23,470 in 2002. The middle 50 percent earned about $34,320. At the opposite ends of the income range, the lowest 10 percent earned less than $13,330, while the highest 10 percent earned more than $106,360.

With the camera rolling, actors from The Young and The Restless *perform a scene under the watchful eye of the director.*

Freedom from Finances

Surviving as an artist is a financial challenge for anyone living solely off his or her art. It takes a lot of thought, determination, and a level head to create a revenue stream that can free up an actor to focus on his or her craft. One of the greatest gifts that an actor may receive is residual income—that is, income generated from work already done. For example, acting in a single commercial that is aired multiple times can earn the actor five, ten, or twenty thousand dollars in a single year, and it allows the possibility of renegotiating the contract and earning additional money during the following year.

An actor can receive residuals from a studio (often for years) for a single day's work on a program that goes into reruns. Actors who seek out work that pays residual income can generate a revenue stream for the future. A regular flow of checks from a number of roles can provide enough for a comfortable living and the freedom to be a full-time actor without the stress of having to work several outside jobs to survive.

Under terms of a contract signed in August 2001, covering all unionized actors, those with speaking parts earned a minimum daily rate of $678, or $2,352 for a five-day week. Actors also receive contributions to their health and pension plans and additional compensation for reruns and foreign telecasts of the productions in which they appear. While union agreements generally determine minimum salaries, any actor or director may negotiate for a salary higher than the minimum. It is important to note, however, that of nearly fifty thousand SAG members only about fifty might be considered stars and therefore have the clout to bargain for higher pay.

More than any other employees in television, actors are the ones who are most widely recognized and credited with the success (or failure) of a show. Any serious actor will admit that performing is exciting, fun, pleasing to the ego, and something that is in the blood. That does not mean that every day's work and every part played satisfies equally, but taken as a whole, most actors would not trade their profession for anything else.

Notes

Chapter 1: Camera Operator

1. David Hand, "How Do I Become a Cameraman?" October 2002. www.tvcameramen.com/lounge/howtobecameraman.htm.

2. Art Kibby, telephone interview by author, May 2004.

3. Yura Monestime, "Artists by Activity," January 2003. www.incard.ca/artistsactivity.htm.

4. Paul Thorman, telephone interview by author, February 2004.

5. Joseph McCarthy, "Filming the World Trade Center Terror Attack," January 2002. www.tvcameramen.com/lounge/photography/photography10.htm.

Chapter 2: Director

6. Laurent Minassian, "What I Do as a Director," January 2003. www.geocities.com/laurentkm2/z3.htm.

7. Quoted in Rob Owen, "Pittsburgh's Hollywood Connection Extends to Television's Directors," March 7, 2004. www.post-gazette.com/pg/04067/281090.stm.

8. Elia Kazan, "On What Makes a Director," 1973. www.actioncutprint.com/kazan.html.

9. Quoted in Owen, "Pittsburgh's Hollywood Connection Extends to Television's Directors."

10. Barbara S. Morris, "Following the Action." www.geocities.com/Morrisbm1/index.htm.

11. Minassian, "What I Do a as Director."

Chapter 3: Producer

12. Gary Reynolds, "Steps to a Fab Job as a Television Producer," www.fabjob.com/tips138.html.

13. NCOSP State, NC, "Television Producer Director II," http://ncosp.osp.state.nc.us/CLASS_SPECS/Spec_Folder_0 3100-04099/PDF_Files/03351.pdf.

14. Bureau of Labor Statistics, U.S. Department of Labor, "Actors, Producers, and Directors," in *Occupational Outlook Handbook, 2004–05 Edition*. www.bls.gov/oco/ocos093. htm.

15. Marvin Konveleski, "Jobs People Love—Television Producer," www.sasknetwork.ca/html/Home/lmi/jpl/jpltv producer.htm.

16. *Princeton Review*, "Career: Television Producer," www.princetonreview.com/cte/profiles/dayInLife.asp?career ID=156.

17. Elizabeth Wilson, "Producer—a Day in the Life," www.college view.com/career/careersearch/job_profiles/mc/pro02. html.

18. Quoted in *Princeton Review*, "Career."

19. *Hobsons College View*, "Producer—Types of Producers," www.collegeview.com/career/careersearch/job_profiles/mc/pro01.html.

20. Konveleski, "Jobs People Love."

21. Quoted in Writers Store Staff, "Interview with Dave Hackel: Creator and Executive Producer of the TV Show *Becker*," February 2001. www.writersstore.com/article.php?articles_id=33.

22. Bureau of Labor Statistics, "Actors, Producers, and Directors."

23. Konveleski, "Jobs People Love."

Chapter 4: Broadcast Engineer

24. Bureau of Labor Statistics, U.S. Department of Labor, "Broadcast and Sound Engineering Technicians and Radio Operators," in *Occupational Outlook Handbook, 2004–05 Edition*. www.bls.gov/oco/ocos109.htm.

25. Jeanne Nagle, *Careers in Television*. New York: Rosen, 2001, p. 59.

26. Bureau of Labor Statistics, "Broadcast and Sound Engineering Technicians and Radio Operators."

27. Paul Thorman, telephone interview by author, July 2004.

28. Streaming Media.com "Broadcast Engineer," October 4, 2000. www.streamingmedia.com/industryjobs/job_detail.asp? job_id=1779.

29. Bureau of Labor Statistics, "Broadcast and Sound Engineering Technicians and Radio Operators."

30. Society of Broadcast Engineers, "SBE Member Jobs Online," 2004. www.sbe.org/jobline.html.

31. Nagle, *Careers in Television*, p. 63.

32. Bureau of Labor Statistics, "Broadcast and Sound Engineering Technicians and Radio Operators."

33. Vernon Stone, "Internships in TV and Radio News: Paid and Unpaid," 1995. www.missouri.edu/~jourvs/interns.html.

34. Shonan Noronha, *Opportunities in Television and Video Careers*. Lincolnwood, IL: VGM, 2003, pp. 70+.

35. Bureau of Labor Statistics, "Broadcast and Sound Engineering Technicians and Radio Operators."

36. Bureau of Labor Statistics, "Broadcast and Sound Engineering Technicians and Radio Operators."

37. Noronha, *Opportunities in Television and Video Careers*, pp. 69–70.

38. Michael K. Powell, "Statements About Digital Television," 2002. http://iwce-mrt.com/ar/radio_fcc_chairman_michael.

Chapter 5: Creative Writer

39. Bureau of Labor Statistics, U.S. Department of Labor, "Writers and Editors," in *Occupational Outlook Handbook, 2004–05 Edition*. www.bls.gov/oco/ocos089.htm.

40. Quoted in Jenna Glatzer, "Interview with Larry Brody," www.absolutewrite.com/screenwriting/larry_brody.htm.

41. Quoted in Bradley J. Morgan and Joseph M. Palmisano, *Film and Video Career Directory*. Detroit: Visible Ink, 1994, p. 12.

42. Cheryl Harris, "Writer in Television," www.museum.tv/ archives/etv/W/htmlW/writerintel/writerintel.htm.

43. Harris, "Writer in Television."

44. siteBytes, "Interview with Stephen Smallwood, TV Producer," www.4cine.co.uk/siteBytes/smallwood/smalltext3.htm.

45. Quoted in Jenna Glatzer, "Interview with Tom Lynch," www.absolutewrite.com/screenwriting/tom_lynch.htm.

46. Quoted in Glatzer, "Interview with Tom Lynch."

47. NBC Career Opportunities, "How to Be a TV Writer," www.nbcjobs.com/How_to_be_a_TV_Writer.html.

48. NBC Career Opportunities, "How to Be a TV Writer."

49. Bureau of Labor Statistics, "Writers and Editors."

50. Bureau of Labor Statistics, "Writers and Editors."

51. Harris, "Writer in Television."

52. Bureau of Labor Statistics, "Writers and Editors."

Chapter 6: Actor

53. Quoted in Morgan and Palmisano, *Film and Video Career Directory*, p. 45.

54. *Daily News*, "Uncowed by Endless Cattle Calls." January 2003. www.nydailynews.com/entertainment/story/50970p-47796c.html.

55. Bureau of Labor Statistics, "Actors, Producers, and Directors."

56. Virginia Education Program, "Acting as a Career," www3.ccps.virginia.edu/career_prospects/briefs/A-D/Actors.html.

57. Bureau of Labor Statistics, "Actors, Producers, and Directors."

58. Bureau of Labor Statistics, "Actors, Producers, and Directors."

59. Bureau of Labor Statistics, "Actors, Producers, and Directors."

60. Actors' Gang, "Los Angeles County Arts Commission Internship," 2004. www.theactorsgang.com/jobs.htm.

Organizations to Contact

Actors Equity Association (AEA)
165 W. Forty-Sixth St., New York, NY 10036
(212) 869-8530
www.actorsequity.org

The AEA is a labor union representing more than forty-five thousand American actors and stage managers working in the professional theater. For ninety years the AEA has negotiated minimum wages and working conditions, administered contracts, and enforced the provisions of various agreements with theatrical employers across the country.

American Federation of Television and Radio Artists (AFTRA)
260 Madison Ave., New York, NY 10016-2401
(212) 532-0800
www.aftra.org/aftra/contact.htm

AFTRA provides funds for education, programs, and research of value to performers, journalists, and recording artists. Resource centers have been established in a number of AFTRA local unions, providing facilities for members to practice their craft and hone their skills.

Broadcast Education Association (BEA)
1771 N St., NW Washington, DC 20036-2891
(202) 429-5354
www.beaweb.org

The BEA is dedicated to helping prepare college students to enter careers in radio and television as well as telecommunications and electronic media. More than thirteen hundred professors, students, and media professionals are currently members of the BEA, and approximately 250 college and university departments and schools are institutional members.

Directors Guild of America (DGA)
7920 Sunset Blvd., Los Angeles, CA 90046

(310) 289-2000

www.dga.org

The DGA is the major group organized to represent directors at all levels in negotiations with the Alliance of Motion Picture and Television Producers in matters of pay, health benefits, creative rights, and other contract issues.

Screen Actors Guild (SAG)

5757 Wilshire Blvd., Los Angeles, CA 90036-3600

(323) 954-1600

www.sag.org

The Screen Actors Guild is the nation's premier labor union representing actors. Established in 1933, SAG exists to enhance actors' working conditions, compensation, and benefits and to be a powerful, unified voice on behalf of artist rights.

Society of Television Engineers

Universal Studios, Inc., Building 480/MZ

Universal City, CA 91608

(818) 777-7778

www.ste-ca.org

The Society of Television Engineers is a Los Angeles–based organization that serves broadcast engineers and manufacturers of television broadcast equipment. The purpose of the society is to provide a common ground for engineering personnel to get together to discuss and solve common technical problems.

Writers Guild of America, West (WGA)

7000 W. Third St., Los Angeles, CA 90048

(323) 951-4000

The WGA promotes and protects the professional and artistic interests of all creators and adaptors of literary material (writers) in the fields of radio, free television, pay television, basic cable television, informational programming, videodiscs/videocassettes, theatrical motion pictures, and other related industries.

For Further Reading

Books

Deborah Perlmutter Bloch, *How to Write a Winning Résumé.* Chicago: VGM Career, 1998. A job-search reference book designed to produce a résumé that will capture an employer's attention.

Richard Bolles, *What Color Is Your Parachute 2002: A Practical Manual for Job-Hunters & Career-Changers.* Berkeley, CA: Ten Speed, 2002. This manual includes information and resources to guide job hunting on the Internet.

Thomas D. Burrows and Donald N. Wood, *Video Production: Disciplines and Techniques.* Burr Ridge, IL: WCB/McGraw-Hill, 2000. This text introduces students to the operations underlying multiple-camera video production. Written in an accessible style that appeals to students, it covers the basics of television production with an emphasis on studio production.

Tanja L. Crouch, *100 Careers in Film and Television.* Hauppauge, NY: Barrons Educational, 2002. A three-hundred-page indepth source of career choices that span both film and the television industry. It includes a list of regional opportunities.

Gary Davis, *Working at a TV Station.* Danbury, CT: Childrens Press, 1998. An introduction to typical (and some untypical) days inside the broadcasting industry by an author who knows what it is like.

Stephen King, *On Writing: A Memoir of the Craft.* New York: Simon & Schuster, 2000. A definitive book on discovering natural writing talent and the basic facts of writing as a career. King personally defines what a writer is and what that person can become.

M.K. Lewis, *Your Film Acting Career: How to Break into the Movies and TV and Survive in Hollywood.* Santa Monica, CA: Gorham House, 1998. This business-of-acting "bible" offers candid, knowledgeable, up-to-date answers to hundreds of questions about finding work in movies, television and commercials; moving to and living in Los Angeles; joining unions; finding an agent; and almost everything else that a newcomer to Hollywood needs to know. Lewis is a Los Angeles acting teacher.

Dan Weaver and Jason Sigel, *Breaking into Television: Proven Advice from Veterans and Interns*. Princeton, NJ: Peterson's, 1998. This book provides valuable insight into what a television career is really like through the eyes of seasoned television veterans (all former interns) and network executives.

Web Sites

AV Video Multimedia Producer (www.avvideo.com). An online magazine that offers articles on electronic and software advances and creative techniques in the production field.

Broadcast Engineering (http://broadcastengineering.primedea business.com). An online magazine for broadcast engineers that provides news of equipment updates and articles on advances in broadcast technology.

Cable World (www.cableworld.com). An online source targeted at cable company executives. This site features analysis, trends, and case studies pertinent to the cable industry.

Digital TV (www.digitaltelevision.com). This electronic magazine explains digital television: its legal ramifications, its history, and its future.

Variety (www.variety.com). An online version of the premier trade publication of the film and television industries, with reviews, news, and commentary.

Videography (www.videography.com). This electronic magazine addresses creative and technical issues of interest to camera operators and contains reviews of video productions.

Works Consulted

Books

John R. Bittner, *Broadcasting: An Introduction*. Englewood Cliffs, NJ: Prentice-Hall, 1980. A popular textbook for students of mass communications. Its chapters cover the history of television, its regulations, and future perspectives. In addition, the reader will learn the economics and the rating systems that drive the industry.

Guide to Literary Agents. Cincinnati: Writers Digest, 1996. Having an agent is not always necessary, but unless the writer is skilled in marketing and the legal elements of being a screenwriter, then that person is advised to find a good agent. The guide lists agents along with their genres, addresses, and what they look for in a client.

Robert L. Hilliard, *Writing for Television and Radio*, 3rd ed. New York: Hastings House. Hilliard's continually updated book addresses the unique world of the broadcast writer, explaining its differences and similarities to other forms of screenwriting.

Bradley J. Morgan and Joseph M. Palmisano, *Film and Video Career Directory*. Detroit: Visible Ink, 1994. A comprehensive guide to what to expect on a job, typical career paths, qualities looked for in an applicant, and unique specialties.

Jeanne Nagle, *Careers in Television*. New York: Rosen, 2001. Nagle explores the primary careers available in the television industry. From actor to reporter to program director, this book discusses job descriptions, education needed to get into those positions, and the salaries those people earn.

Shonan Noronha, *Opportunities in Television and Video Careers*. Lincolnwood, IL: VGM, 2003. The author is an internationally known authority on mass media communications. His book covers a variety of careers, including those in creative, technical, sales, and marketing fields, as well as how to have a successful job search.

J. Michael Straczynski, *The Complete Book of Scriptwriting*. Cincinnati: Synthetic Worlds, 1996. Straczynski, the executive producer and head writer for the *Babylon 5* series and a writer for *Murder, She Wrote,* the *New Twilight Zone,* and many other successful programs, shares much of his success as a scriptwriter.

Periodicals

Gregory Miller, "Ten Steps to a Snappier Script," *Writer's Digest,* 2000.

Editorial Staff, "Where to Sell Manuscripts," *The Writer,* Boston 2004.

Internet Sources

Actors' Gang, "Los Angeles County Arts Commission Internship," 2004. http://www.theactorsgang.com/jobs.htm.

Bureau of Labor Statistics, U.S. Department of Labor, "Actors, Producers, and Directors," *Occupational Outlook Handbook 2004-05 Edition.* www.bls.gov/oco/ocos093.htm.

———, U.S. Department of Labor, "Broadcast and Sound Engineering Technicians and Radio Operators," in *Occupational Outlook Handbook, 2004–05 Edition.* www.bls.gov/oco/ocos109.htm.

Bureau of Labor Statistics, "Writers and Editors," in *Occupational Outlook Handbook, 2004–05 Edition.*

———, U.S. Department of Labor, "Writers and Editors," in *Occupational Outlook Handbook, 2004–05 Edition.* www.bls.gov/oco/ocos089.htm.

Collegeboard, "Broadcast Technicians," 2004. www.collegeboard.com/apps/careers/0,3477,30-110,00.html.

Cox Communications, "Search Jobs," 2004. www.cox.com/CoxCareer/search.asp.

Daily News, "Uncowed by Endless Cattle Calls," January 2003. www.nydailynews.com/entertainment/story/50970p-47796c.html.

Jenna Glatzer, "Interview with Larry Brody," www.absolutewrite.com/screenwriting/larry_brody.htm.

———, "Interview with Tom Lynch," www.absolutewrite.com/screenwriting/tom_lynch.htm.

David Hand, "How Do I Become a Cameraman?" October 2002. www.tvcameramen.com/lounge/howtobecameraman.htm.

Cheryl Harris, "Writer in Television," www.museum.tv/archives/etv/W/htmlW/writerintel/writerintel.htm.

Hobsons College View, "Producer—Types of Producers," www.college view.com/career/careersearch/job_profiles/mc/pro01.html.

Elia Kazan, "On What Makes a Director," 1973. www.actioncut print.com/kazan.html.

Marvin Konveleski, "Jobs People Love—Television Producer," www.sasknetwork.ca/html/Home/lmi/jpl/jpltvproducer.htm.

Linda McAlister, "So You Want to Be an Actor?" 1996–2004. www.mcalistertalent.com/be-actor.htm.

Joseph McCarthy, "Filming the World Trade Center Terror Attack," January 2002. www.tvcameramen.com/lounge/photo graphy/photography10.htm.

Laurent Minassian, "What I Do as a Director," January 2003. www.geocities.com/laurentkm2/z3.htm.

Yura Monestime, "Artists by Activity," January 2003. www.incard. ca/artistsactivity.htm.

Barbara S. Morris, "Following the Action." www.geocities.com/Morrisbm1/index.htm.

NBC Career Opportunities, "How to Be a TV Writer," www.nbc jobs.com/How_to_be_a_TV_Writer.html.

NCOSP State, NC, "Television Producer Director II," http://ncosp.osp.state.nc.us/CLASS_SPECS/Spec_Folder_03100-04 099/PDF_Files/03351.pdf.

Rob Owen, "Pittsburgh's Hollywood Connection Extends to Television's Directors," March 7, 2004. www.post-gazette. com/pg/04067/281090.stm.

Michael K. Powell, "Statements About Digital Television," 2002. http://iwce-mrt.com/ar/radio_fcc_chairman_Michael.

Princeton Review, "Career: Television Producer," www.princeton review.com/cte/profiles/dayInLife.asp?careerID=156.

Gary Reynolds, "Steps to a Fab Job as a Television Producer," www.fabjob.com/tips138.html.

Schools in the USA, "Television System Engineer," 2004. www. schoolsintheusa.com/careerprofiles_details.cfm?CarID=138.

siteBytes, "Interview with Stephen Smallwood, TV Producer," www.4cine. co.uk/siteBytes/smallwood/smalltext3.htm.

Society of Broadcast Engineers, "SBE Member Jobs Online," 2004. www.sbe.org/jobline.html.

Vernon Stone, "Internships in TV and Radio News: Paid and Unpaid," 1995. www.missouri.edu/~jourvs/interns.html.

Streaming Media.com "Broadcast Engineer," October 4, 2000. www. streamingmedia.com/industryjobs/job_detail.asp?job_id=1779.

Richard Toscan, *The Playwriting Seminars: The Full-Length Play*, 1995–2003. www.pubinfo.vcu.edu/artweb/playwriting/tv.html.

TV Cameramen, "How TV Cameramen Protect Themselves While Covering Riots," October 2000. www.tvcameramen. com/lounge/israelriots04.htm.

TV Museum, "Producer in Television." www.museum.tv/ archives/etv/P/htmlP/producerint/producerint.htm.

UCI Series Concepts, "Television Engineer," May 1998. www. hr.uci.edu/uc-ser/e/20/aa2-20.html.

Virginia Education Program, "Acting as a Career." www3.ccps. virginia.edu/career_prospects/briefs/A-D/Actors.html.

Vocational Information Center, "Electronics Career Guide," 2003. www.khake.com/page19.html.

Elizabeth Wilson, "Producer—a Day in the Life," www.college view.com/career/careersearch/job_profiles/mc/pro02.html.

Writers Store Staff, "Interview with Dave Hackel: Creator and Executive Producer of the TV Show *Becker*," February 2001. www.writersstore.com/article.php?articles_id=33.

XAP, "Creative Writers," 2004.www.xap.com/Career/careerdetail/ career27-3043.02.html.

Index

Picture Credits

About the Author

R.T. Byrum began his career as a disc jockey before graduating with a bachelor of fine arts degree in broadcast communications. His postgraduate work was at the University of Southern California, where he studied motion picture production techniques under some of the industry's top professionals. He later taught advanced radio and television communications at both Northern Kentucky University and Southern Ohio College, and he was a visiting professor at the University of Cincinnati and Xavier University. Byrum's broadcasting credits include videographer, news reporter, anchorman, children's program host, creative writer, producer, and director of a number of local and nationally syndicated television programs. He is the author of seven young adult novels and is the current president of the Christian Authors Guild based in Atlanta, Georgia. He and his wife, Karen, have three adult sons (Tom, Jonathan, and David), two grandsons, and a miniature dachshund named Angel. He lives in historic Marietta, Georgia, where he finds much of his inspiration for his novels.